Other Books by John D. Carter

Intelligence and Attention

Intimacy in Cocktail Lounges

Cape Lazo

Crazy Cousins

Belle Islet Lady

Banny's Boys

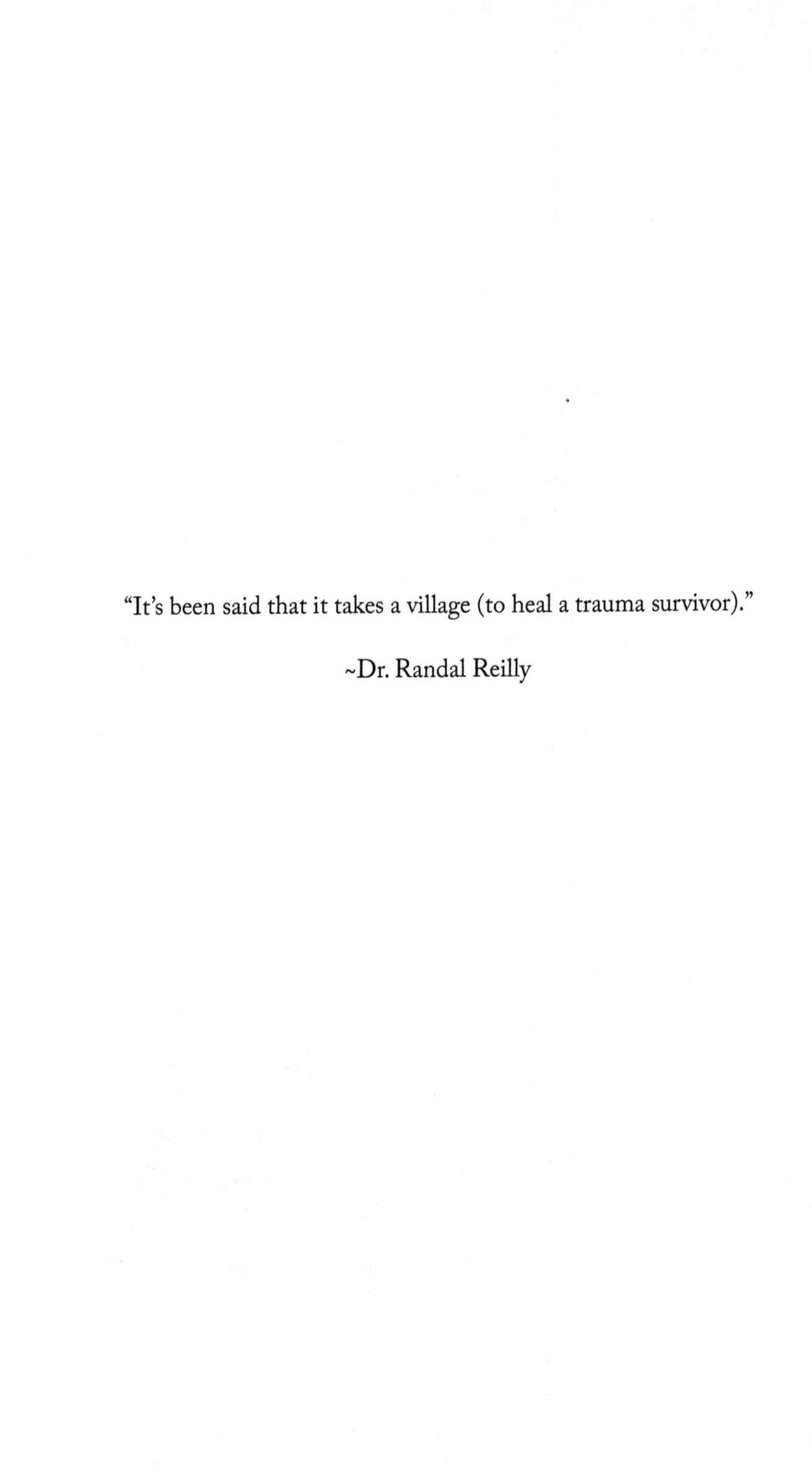

"It's been said that it takes a village (to heal a trauma survivor)."

~Dr. Randal Reilly

Shane's Coma

Dr. Reilly Travels to India

by

John D. Carter

Book and cover design: Vladimir Verano, VertVolta Design

Cover images:
creative commons ⓒ kritesh-kaushik via Pexels.com
creative commons ⓒ Mao via Pexels.com
creative commons ⓒ CDC via Pexels.com

Published by

John D. Carter

print ISBN: 978-0-9940346-8-7
ebook ISBN: 978-0-9940346-9-4

Author contact:
Belle.Islet@gmail.com

Table of Contents

"When you are running the marathon, it's not all
the miles before the finish line that wears you down,
sometimes it's the pebble in your shoe."

~Dr. Randal Reilly

Part One

INTRO

"The great fault of all ethics hitherto has been that they believed themselves to have to deal only with the relations of human with humans. In reality, however, the question is what is our attitude to the world and all life that comes within our reach."

~Albert Schweitzer (1875 – 1965)

Shane's in a Coma

Really don't know why I answer the telephone at two in the morning, but seems like I always do. It's never good news at that time of night. Should've just let the call go to voicemail. Shouldn't even have the stupid phone by my bed on the nightstand in the first place. Ringer should be off, or set do not disturb.

I hear three rings chime out, and call display shows my sister's name, thumbnail picture, and phone number. Of course, I have to answer her two o'clock call because this is often a reflection of the old proverb: A stitch in time saves nine.

"Hi Annette, what's up?" I asked groggily.

"Shane is in a *coma*!"

"What?" I woke up quickly.

Shane Bighill is my nephew Ned's best friend. "How did that happen? He's got less than six months left on his prison sentence!"

"Yes, I knew that," she sighed loudly with some exasperation and anguish. "The Warden's Assistant called me because I am listed as the lawyer of record on Shane's prison file."

"They called you at two in the morning?"

"No, actually, they called earlier. I've been trying to get ahold of Ned."

I scoffed out loud, "Ned *never* answers his phone."

"I know," she exhaled harshly. "I left him voicemail, and a text telling him to call back ASAP."

"Okay, that's a good plan," I said with a cajoling mocking tone.

Annette wheezed, "Just wondering about Amelia. She's still not taking any of my calls. So, if it's two in the morning here in Vancouver that means it's two in the afternoon in India. Amelia will answer if *you* call. I can't call her. You know, she'll see it's my name on the call display. And if I use any call display duplicity measures or tricks that will set her off the *Anger-Richter Scale*. You call, okay? She needs to know."

"No," I answered, maybe a little more forcibly than needed, "I'm not calling Amelia for you. I can't get involved with your mother-daughter dramatics!"

"C'mon, she'll answer, or at least listen to the message if it is you or Ned calling."

"Annette, listen, don't try and get someone else to call Amelia to say Shane's in a coma," I moaned. "And it's not for *me* to call Amelia. *You* have to do it. You two have to start speaking to each other. Get it together, will you please."

Then she snorted, with more noise than necessary, "I *have called*! Raj says she doesn't want to speak with me, and she deletes my messages without even listening to them."

I shook my head and smiled. Raj is my niece Amelia's new husband. Amelia did not really want to get married, but in order to live in India, with Raj, it was the best, if not the *only* option open to both of them. Culture, Raj's family, Indian traditions and all those things make everyday life a little easier. Besides, they certainly were in love.

Historically, and even at the best of times, I do not like to get involved with their mother-daughter squabbles. This current phase has been difficult for more than a while. It's not good. I'm sure they will sort it out at some point. The mother-daughter branch on the family tree bends, but doesn't break. Well, not yet there's still some distance to travel.

Families, permutations and imperfections.

Time Travellers

"Knowing is one thing, and understanding is another matter." – Albert Einstein (1879 – 1955)

Mathematically, this will be my third trip to India. Of course, the first two sojourns count, but they were markedly different in that I was accompanying my wife, Harjit. And although Harjit left India at the young age of seven, immigrating to Vancouver, she does still speak fluent Punjabi, Hindi, Urdu, and, importantly, she understands many more cultural traditions and nuances than I do.

I speak what is often commonly called elementary *Punglish*—it's a combo of vernacular English and poor Punjabi. My gestures are also another issue. Besides all that, I'm extremely left-handed, too. Handedness is neurological, but that's another narrative.

My wife, Harjit, works as an appeals court judge, and I know from scanning our shared family calendar, she is tied up for the next *six* weeks with another big, complicated court case. Thus, I have decided that I am going to travel solo because history suggests six weeks sometimes morphs into eight or ten. By then the Indian weather will have turned, it will be too hot to travel in the Punjab. Besides, ethically, morally, and whatever other flag you fly, I simply can't wait any longer to tell Amelia and Raj about Shane's coma. They needed to know yesterday, but I did not want to telephone. This is *not* a phone call delivery type of a message. So, I am going in person. Of course, Shane could come out of the coma at any time, or on the other hand, this coma might take some time, too. Either way, I've got to go tell Amelia. Of course, nobody but me thinks this trip to India is a good idea. And, of course, you know it's not the first time that's happened. Families and their histories can get so convoluted, complicated, and crazy.

So, there I was, patiently sitting in the corner of the documents processing waiting room in the Vancouver Office of the Consulate of India to obtain a foreign traveller's visa, I could feel my new phone vibrating in my pocket. Thankfully, the ringer was off, I did not answer, and just let it go to transcript voicemail.

I love my new cellular phone/minicomputer gadget. It is good. This thing has voicemail with simultaneous transcripts. I prefer to read rather than listen to long voicemail messages. I'm a good reader. I can even read *between* the lines. I can comprehend the gist from the writing. Auditory processing issues are another thing altogether, especially when someone prattles on without getting to the point. "Oh, was that a hitch in her voice?"

Standard voice mail has too many drawbacks, but my new phone with simultaneous voice-to-text transcripts has been helpful with patients and family calls. Nuisance calls are another matter altogether.

I pushed the voicemail transcript button:

"Hey, Uncle R," it was my nephew, "it's Ned calling. Call me back, please. Mum says you're going to India. I gotta talk to you about Shane. You know, they're changing from sails to steam, and what it all means. See ya soon baboon. Call me, okay."

Smiling, shaking my head, I thought, "Oh that Ned, he is a live wire." Just then my number was flashed on the big screen at the front of the reception room. It was time to go the next processing station. The process goes one step at a time. I've been here before.

At the next passport processing station, a lovely young lady took the envelope with all my supporting documents. She thumbed through each page and said, "You need to sign and date on this line."

I signed, dated, and said thank you in Punjabi, "Shukria, dhannvaad."

She smiled, "Here is your interview file and number. You need to take this, go down that hall, turn left and take a seat in the large waiting room."

Whew, this means I made it through station one. The next waiting room was much larger than the first station. I looked around and there was a lot of people already seated waiting for their number to be called. Vancouver sends a lot of people to India. It's a busy place.

Up at the front of the room there were two big screens with letters and numbers scrolling. My small piece of paper had **D53** stamped on it. The screen showed **A17, B43, C20,** and **D22** were on deck. Of course, I had no idea has fast this process was going to take. Two years ago, I had arrived early in the morning and the process was quite quick. Right now, it was almost noon so who knows. I took a seat in the back corner. I wondered whether they shut down for lunch break.

Leaning back in the consulate chair, I sighed with a big relief to be getting this passport travel visa task done, and I consciously closed my eyes, just for a moment or two.

Otto Warmbier

"The past is beautiful because one never realizes an emotion
at the time. It expands later, and thus we don't have
complete emotions about the present, only about the past."
~Virginia Woolf (1882 – 1941)

"Dr. Reilly, are you sleeping?"

~

Frankly, I still can't grasp the idea of Shane Bighill lying in a coma at the old Fort Saskatchewan Prison Hospital. I'm still not clear on how it happened in the first place. My sister Annette is a highfalutin downtown lawyer, and she is *aggressively* taking steps to have Shane transferred to her preferred physicians at Vancouver General Hospital. "If you will not listen to me, perhaps a court order and a large lawsuit *might* change your mind."

Although the prison lawyers were not sure about the shitstorm descending on them, you knew they were worried. There's nothing quite like my sister coming at you full tilt. History shows, it can be concerning. It's always about the evidence.

My niece, Amelia, has more than once commented on the lawyerly dissimilarity between when her mother is *assertive* as contrasted with *aggressive*. "There is a big difference, you need to know when to keep your powder dry, and when to shoot. It's not semantics!" Their adversarial system works differently than the one I live in—I'm a social scientist.

I remember this American kid, Otto Warmbier, from Ohio, who was a university student visiting North Korea as a tourist in

January 2016. Otto was arrested and convicted for attempting to steal a propaganda poster from the hallway wall of his hotel. All the mainstream news and social media channels showed the video of Otto taking down the poster hundreds of times. The television showed the Korean courtroom footage of Otto pleading for forgiveness and asking mercy. This was dramatic, and painful to watch.

For his crime of trying to steal a poster, which read, "Let's arm ourselves strongly with Kim Jong-Un's patriotism!" Otto was sentenced to fifteen years imprisonment with hard labour. They led him sobbing out of the courtroom his legs like wet noodles. It was heartbreaking.

A couple weeks after his sentencing, Otto lapsed into a coma. However, the Korean authorities didn't tell anyone about the coma until many months later in *June* 2017. It took the government some seventeen months after his imprisonment to say Otto was in a coma. The Koreans claimed Otto's comatose state was due to a sleeping pill and botulism.

In our case, at least we found out about Shane's comatose state straight away. The authorities were not hiding him. Nevertheless, the circumstances and cause of Shane's coma are still not clear, yet. My sister is on their case, and she is relentless. It's a type of mama bear madness with her. Grizzly on the loose.

Eventually, Otto was repatriated and flown back to the United States, still in a coma, but only to die six days after returning home. Otto never regained consciousness and died June 19, 2017. He couldn't self-report the cause or conditions. The American medical team could not find *any* evidence of botulism in Otto's body. Officially, the Cincinnati Coroner's report was unable to identify a specific cause of death.

Sure, hope Shane pulls through, this coma stuff…

-~-

Something poked my arm. I felt it again. It was harder this time.

"Hey, mister, Ned's uncle," a voice was beckoning. "Wake up man, you are snoring!"

I sat up with a startle. "Hello."

"Hey man, you were snoring too loud. What's your number? Hope you didn't sleep through your call." She grabbed the piece of paper out of my hand. "You're **D53.** The screen's got **D49** now. You are close."

"Sorry," I shook my head, "I can't remember your name?" Although she did look familiar, I didn't really know who this person is poking me in the arm. I ventured forth saying, "I'm Dr. Reilly. And you are?"

"I'm Parm Gill!" She said with some strength, "I'm Raj's sister. I work in Nina Bighill's lab at UBC. We've met before, but you don't remember me, right?"

"Oh, yes, yes, yes, of course, I said nodding my head. Trying to connect the dots, I asked, "Do I call you Parm or Parminder?"

"You can call me Parm, Parminder, Minder, PKG or whatever you want, but don't call me a Paki. That's a slur; my people are from the Punjab. Oh hey, look at the screen **D53,** that's your number. Go; don't make them wait because it puts 'em in a mood. Go!"

Stumbling towards to the front for my travel visa interview processing, I turned and gave a limp wave-type salute to Parminder.

"Thanks," I said softly.

Parminder Kaur Gill

"You are known by your manners, not your name."
~Harjinder Kaur Bahia Sidhu (1943 – 2018)

So, there I am sitting, deep down in the bowels of the Consulate of India in their downtown Vancouver office. I need their passport validation update, and this is the place where it happens. I am a Canadian citizen by birth, but with deep family roots in the Punjab. Indian roots, the officials like that at the consulate. I have all the appropriate documents assembled, labelled, and in transparent folder holders, thanks to my mother—the queen of document organization.

Okay, here's the situation, Chaachee, my auntie, has died from extreme old age. In our family honouring tradition, this means I must travel to India (even though I do not want to go). And, yes, I have told them so.

Chaachee was my father's sister, and although my memory of her is fuzzy, I think I do remember her, sort of, but not well. It was a long time ago when I was around five years old the last time, I saw her. That was eighteen years ago now. Doesn't matter anyway because family duties, obligations, and my father's dictates determine the deal. I am going to India. Can't get out of it. It's my *duty*.

My parents already left Vancouver for India nine days ago to attend the first phase of the Antam Sanskaar. It's a Sikh final rites cremation ceremony that celebrates the completion of life. My parents are quite religious, I am not, and just the same I go along to get along. Indian family life is like that.

I am going to the next part of the completion of life ceremony where the cremation ashes are spread in the river Punjab. Sikhs don't do tombstones, crypts or monuments for the dead. We send the ashes back to a river. Sikhs return to mother earth.

We have relatives and family friends from all over the diaspora returning for this end-of-life celebration. This will be my first time doing this thing. It's all applied anthropology and religion as far as I am concerned. Nevertheless, I'm most respectful and Auntie deserves the love and honours. It's the least I can do. She was a good woman.

My older brother, Raj, currently lives in India. He is a well-paid research scientist at the Punjab University. When I get there, Raj is supposed to travel with me, and drive us to the old gurdwara temple by the river. That will be helpful, as I'd rather go as a duet than travel solo. Women travelling solo in India is *never* a good idea. Besides our father would go nuts with me travelling solo. Father is already disconsolate with Raj marrying a *white* girl. Me, on the other hand, I like his wife. I knew her from the University of British Columbia. Amelia is cool, smart, and headstrong. No one pushes her around. She holds a medical degree *and* a law degree. My bro married a brainiac.

My departure to India was delayed because I had exams to write at the university. My father values education and feels nothing is more important than exams. If I missed exams that would be unconscionable, as far as father is concerned. Certainly, a death in the family would have warranted an authorized UBC exam exemption with no strings attached. Nonetheless, I was eager to complete the exams and move forward with my studies.

Currently, I'm attending some interesting seminars with some professors doing cutting edge stuff and it's got us all fired up. Professor Bruno Zamburn just taught us how to do statistical structural equation models. I didn't get it at first, too confusing, and a bit like black magic. Mind you, my friend Kelsey Pearce said the same thing about calculus *and* matrix algebra. We got through that together. In the end it wasn't so difficult once we re-framed the whole thing into understandable chunks. Theory construction starts to become a real possibility. Kelsey is so smart. She doesn't have to work as I do. She says, "Don't sweat small stuff, Parm. It's just tortoise and hare principles. Nothing to it, and for sure you can do it!"

Kelsey says when people are discouraged, they won't do too much, but encouragement will move them along faster and farther. Kelsey is *always* encouraging.

Last semester we took a child development course with Dr. Emily Leonard. She showed us videos of social psychology experiments that propose language is neurologically "hard wired" into the brain's parietal lobe. They had two groups of two-year olds. One group were clearly premorbid autistic children, and the other was randomly selected "normal" kids.

The videos show the child and mother coming into the lab's research room one at a time. Dr. Leonard would put a small pile of foaming shaving cream on the kid's hand. The baby two-year olds have limited language skills. Basically, they don't talk, but the autistic child would either wipe the cream off or gaze at the hand. In sharp contrast the *normal* randomly selected kid would engage the mother and researcher by showing the cream on the hand with a smile or gesture. From this the hypothesis of hardwired language was developed.

When I return from India, I have been hired to work as a research assistant in Dr. Leonard's lab. It's just basic low paying graduate student wage work, but the experience will be awesome. And it's interesting stuff. I need a decent thesis topic, plus a supervisor, and this might have some potential. Nothing ventured nothing gained, who knows this could pan out.

Additionally, I also have another UBC part-time job working in Nina Bighill's lab as a grad student research assistant. I've been working there for a few years. My brother Raj got me the job initially and I did the rest meritocratically.

Amelia Reilly was in charge of the lab when I first started working there. Six degrees of separation, or whatever you want to call it, now Raj and Amelia are married living in India. Even Einstein said time was hard to understand.

All of a sudden, I can hear this old white guy sitting in the corner snoring loudly like a freight train. When I looked closer, I realized the old guy snoring is Ned and Amelia Reilly's uncle. I've seen him around at Reilly soireés, but I don't really know him very well. At any rate, I had to do something. If he slept through his number call that would be bad, so I walked over and lightly poked his arm. At first, he wouldn't wake up. So, I poked him again, a bit harder this time.

"Hey, Ned's uncle," I said trying get him to stir. "Wake up, you are snoring!"

Finally, he sat up with a startle. "Hello," he said somewhat groggily.

"Hey man, you were snoring too loud. What's your number? Hope you didn't sleep through your call." I reached for the piece of paper in his hand. "You're **D53.** The screen's got **D49** now. You are close."

"Sorry," he shook his head, "I can't remember your name? I'm Dr. Reilly."

"I'm Parm Gill!" I said with some strength, "I'm Raj's sister. I work in Nina Bighill's lab at UBC. We've met before, but you don't remember me, right?"

"Oh, yes, yes, yes, of course," he said nodding his head. Obviously, he was trying to connect the dots. He asked, "Do I call you Parm or Parminder?"

"You can call me Parm, Parminder, Minder, PKG or whatever you want, but don't call me a Paki. That's a slur; my people are from the Punjab. Oh hey, look at the screen, **D53,** that's your number. Go; don't make them wait because it puts 'em in a mood. Go!" I flapped my hands waving him on his way to the front.

He stood up and wobbled towards the front, turned, lifted his hand and seemed to softly say, "Thanks."

Demented or Delinquency

"A candle loses nothing by lighting another candle."
~James Keller (1900 – 1977)

Every now and then I sometimes misplace my phone. I don't do it *all the time*, just every now and then. Today, finally, after rummaging all around the whole house, I found the stupid device in my jacket pocket, the lucky jacket I wore yesterday. Unfortunately, I'm now in the habit of leaving the ringer tuned off, so no sense calling my own number. I know I need to get someone to show me how to download the find my phone app. That's another item on the list of things to do—soon.

The list keeps growing.

I fired up the phone to the home screen. There were a bunch of messages, emails, and whatnot indications. Four calls, and three messages, were from nephew Ned. I knew I had best deal with these first off before anything else. I pushed the play button:

First Message:

"Hey, Uncle R, it's Ned, I'm calling you, *again*. Now I've got people calling me about *you*. Raj's little sister Parmy G says she saw you at the passport office and you were acting weird. What's with that? I told her not to think anything of it. I explained that I have an elderly eccentric uncle. Remember what I told you, don't be weird. Especially in public."

Second Message:

"Hey, it's me again, calling you for the *third* time. Answer your phone. Call me back. Don't make me put my mum on your case."

~

Ned's mother is my sister Annette, and she's been on my case all my life. She calls it a "sister's prerogative." I called Ned back only to engage in another round of telephone tag. I left him a message.

"Hi Ned, got your message, and I'm calling you back. Yes, I saw Raj's sister, Parminder, at the passport place. I guess I nodded off, started snoring, and she woke me in time to get the documents processed. Any who, now, I'm good to go. Flying out on Friday. Talk to you soon baboon."

~

All my family is showing way more concern over me than is necessary. It's all been overblown and is now way out of proportion. My mental state is just fine, for the most part, thanks. After all, I'm almost officially a senior citizen. In Canada, age sixty-five earns senior citizen status. That's when they put you on the Canada Pension Plan. It's a good thing.

In terms of social antecedents, this whole thing seemed to get started when we had a family dinner at my sister's house last month. While passing the chicken casserole my sister, Annette, casually mentions, "I hear your old friend Arthur Sutherland has been having some tough times, eh?"

Maybe I might have overreacted a bit, but Arthur is one my old friends from university days and I felt sympathetic towards his current difficulties. "Oh, great, so much for lawyer/client confidentiality!" I snorted. "You are just as bad as the social media wretches."

"You are confused, Arthur's not *my* client," Annette shrieked. "He's appeared in open court, and there is no publication ban. Mainstream media has been reporting his case everywhere. They're talking about it on television, talk radio and the newspapers."

"Fake news." Ned chirps in much louder than helpful.

I could see Nina nudging Ned under the table to signal he should cool it. Much to my sister's consternation, Ned and Nina have been living together ever since Nina's twin brother Shane was incarcerated for manslaughter four years ago.

"No Ned," I sighed. "Unfortunately, it's not fake news, Arthur has admitted to committing some professional misbehaviours."

"They can't put you in jail for that, can they?" Ned asked with a side-glance to Nina for reassurance.

"No, I don't know about jail time, but it is more than likely he will lose his psychologist's license, at a minimum."

Ned snorted, "Wow, he kisses a couple of patients, and loses his shrink's license? That's gotta suck."

"Sucks for who?" Nina asks. "Maybe the patients feel something about that?"

Sensing some increasing dinnertime tension, I thought it might be helpful to lower the room's temperature. "Well, Ned," I was getting started, "I don't think it's a simple as a couple of unwanted kisses. Even so, unsolicited patient kissing is completely wrong."

Before I could continue confabulating, Annette just had to blurt, "I understand a little more than *non-consenting* kissing has been alleged. After all, Arthur was formally *charged* with sexual assault."

Ned whistled, "Ouch, sexual assault sounds serious, Uncle R. What's with that?"

"One of the victims, her identity and name are court protected, claims Arthur fondled her while she was hypnotized." I shook my head.

"Victims, plural?" Ned asked. "How many *were* there?"

"At this point there are three women who have come forward to say Arthur acted inappropriately when they were his patients."

"Ouch!" I could see Nina nudge Ned under the table, again. He flinched. "What?" Ned looked at Nina with a confused expression.

Nina tilted her head, and simply said, "Please pass the biryani." At that point Ned knew it was time to talk about the weather or anything, but Arthur Sutherland's current situation.

Still, although all these allegations and admissions are confusing for me, I felt bad for Arthur. He's an old friend. There was a time when we saw each other every day. We were classmates. We played squash twice a week, drank beer afterwards, and enjoyed each other's company. We were best of friends. Artie was my study buddy. He got me over some steep academic hills that had tough stuff with complicated course materials. Artie made mathematical statistics make sense. I got it. The light went on, shone brightly. I couldn't have done all that stuff without him.

A happy memory was when we both took the Level One Clinical Hypnotism training course at a symposium in Banff. Truth is, I only went because it was Banff. The Alberta symposium was the reason for going. Truth be told, I was mostly there just to ski Mt. Norquay. This sojourn was way better than the time we took the Rolfing course in Santa Monica. Mind you, although Primal Rolfing was not for me, it wasn't a total waste of money or training time, because we stayed at Arthur's family beach house, and his sister, Nicole, taught me how to surf. Nicky did some cooking, too.

Arthur was completely enamoured with hypnotism as a treatment for patients with eating disorders, depression, anxiety, and even PTSD. For him it was a clinical crescent wrench. He became a hypnotism paradigm *disciple.* Artie kept taking more courses, attended fancy symposiums, in exciting cities, and took supervised training from the great gurus.

Historically, I was always skeptical of hypnotism's clinical power, but Arthur was my friend, he was a believer, and that was fine with me. I preferred traditional, straight forward, evidence-based therapies like Cognitive Behavioural Treatments, which easily received funding and third-party co-payments without hassles. Bread and butter methods made more sense to me. Besides, I had a mortgage to pay. All the Employee Assistance Programs wanted to know how long someone was likely to be off the job with a psychological problem. Hypnotism was a little looser, harder to develop therapy goals, but Arthur didn't care. He was a believer.

A year or so after graduation, Arthur took a lucrative position with the renowned Hypnosis Institute of Waikiki. Consequently, we didn't see each other as often after his move. Three years ago, he got divorced, again, and decided it was time to come back to Canada.

Time had taken a hard toll on Arthur. Aging is not necessarily linear for any of us, yet Arthur had not aged well. Too much drinking, smoking, and a poor diet never help. Arthur had developed some health issues. We reconnected when he returned to East Vancouver. At first, we saw each other regularly for a while, and then not so much. He was busy establishing a new psychology practice. I was busy doing my thing, too. Life is like that. We had drifted into different lanes. Arthur always quoted John Lennon: "Life is what happens while you are making future plans."

The last time I saw Arthur was a couple months ago, before the scandal broke. We had lunch at posh place downtown. Usually, I can't drink too much at lunchtime because doing so sabotages the afternoon, and then I need a nap. Arthur ordered a bottle of fancy bourgeois French wine.

"You look good Randy." Arthur said as we clinked wine glasses. "Wish I had paid better attention to my health. It's all catching up with me in my old age now."

Wrinkled my brow and I shook my head. "Art, what the fuck are you talking about? *Old age*, we are both sixty-three years old. That's nothing!"

"Well, no, not really," Arthur took a sip of wine. "Sixty-three is old enough to be diagnosed with premorbid demented senility."

"What?" I about choked on my antipasto. I was flabbergasted, gobsmacked. "Who says you have dementia?"

Arthur tilted his head and grimaced, "Dr. Winston Quan at the UBC hospital's Brain Centre Clinic diagnosed me a couple weeks ago. I'm going back later this week for follow-ups."

Arthur went on to explain that it didn't happen overnight. "Randy, you remember how Professor Oldridge described mental illness like smoke coming under the door?"

Disclosures are a familiar and frequent occurrence in my psychology practice. It happens all the time, even so, Arthur's self-report took the wind out of my sails. "What the hell are you talking about, Arthur?"

"You know how smoke slides in under the door and fills the room. You don't know it's too late, until it is too late. Smoke inhalation gets you that way. Same with senile dementia."

Who was I to argue or try and defend or deny his diagnosis?

Arthur raised his index finger to get the waiter's attention. "Garcon, another bottle of wine, please."

Okay, *another* bottle of wine, whatever. I rode a Brompton folding bicycle to the restaurant because of the downtown parking problems. Who knew about riding home after *two* bottles of wine with lunch? Wasn't planning for that part.

Who was it that said, "What soberness conceals, drunkenness reveals?"

Artie, "Freud."

Raj ~ Family Duties and Decisions

"Givers have to set limits because takers rarely do."
~Henry Ford (1863 – 1947)

I was happy to hear my sister, Parminder, was coming to India for a visit. I was not quite so happy to hear about all the other family duties dumped on me, but that was typical. I'm her older brother. My family is all about *duties*.

"Raj," my mother had left a message on my phone. "You are picking Parminder up at the Delhi airport, right? And a good car, too. No junky car." One time I met my mother at the airport in a borrowed, compact, older model car. Matta ji was not happy that day and going forward she just won't let me live it down.

"Ma, don't worry, I'll get a good car for Parmy."

Now it seems, Chaachee, out auntie, has died from extreme old age, and that means we must attend the Antam Sanskaar just outside the large industrial city of Ludhiana. No problem, although I am not as religiously devout as the rest of my family, I can pick up Parmy at the Delhi airport and deliver her to Ludhiana. Whether or not I stay and get involved with all the events depends on my father. If he is magnanimous when we meet for the first time since we said angry goodbyes, I will consider staying. If he acts like an asshole, then I'm out of there. I don't need his old school bulltweed and Indo-buckwas. He doesn't know everything.

Unlike my mother and Parmy, who have always had a close relationship, my father and I have a rocky past. It started when I was a kid and just continues to this day. I never worry about measuring up to his expectations. Traditional values don't mean much to me. The father/son thing is just a relative concept. Likely, I'm closer to mother anyway, she is easier to talk to, and she listens. Pops preaches.

Five years ago, when I was attending university in the Punjab, my father went absolutely beserkoe nuts over my decision to take a break from studying. In my mind I just felt like I had to return to Vancouver and support my childhood friend, Shane Bighill. He had been charged with *second-degree murder*. I had to be there to support Shane. It was a no-brainer for me, but Pops had to go ahead and act like he had no brain. He couldn't have been less supportive if he tried. We constantly clashed. It was a terrible time between us. Then it was the silent treatment.

Right when I was feeling down about the family's identity and cultural composition, Parm disclosed that I wasn't the first born in our family. Mum had a stillbirth before me. I had no idea and could only imagine what that must have been like for my mother. Maybe that is why she is much more pragmatic than Pops, life has always been different for her. Pops thinks he's the boss of everyone. He knows it all.

For sure, I have no need for Pop's approval. My mother's acceptance is a different story.

The Days Behind Us

Harvard's Ralph Waldo Emerson (1803 – 1882) said,
"Health is the first wealth."

"Good morning Randal," I knew it was unlikely that he would be in his office this early, so I purposely left him voicemail, "Arthur here, nice to see you yesterday. Hope you arrived home safely. You looked a little wobbly wonky on that fancy bicycle. Let's get together again soon, shall we. Give me a call to sort it. Cheers."

Randy Reilly and I have been friends since the beginning of time, so it seems. We met when we were first-year doctoral students at UBC. We had a luncheon rendezvous yesterday, and the remarkable thing about our friendship is that time doesn't matter. We simply pick up where we left off. Randy is like a brother from another mother. Everyone says, "Randy, he's a good guy."

Yesterday, over lunch, I disclosed my premorbid dementia senility diagnosis. Randy was shocked, demanded I seek a second opinion. He was dismayed when I told him Dr. Quan; from the UBC Brain Centre was the *third* opinion. Dr. Quan's diagnosis was definitive and evidenced-based. Hard to argue with the brain scan pictures. In California, previously, they just said what they thought I should hear with a sketchy prognosis. Dr. Quan was the opposite. Canadian health care is superior, unless you are a rich American.

Thought I should also let Randy know it was likely some mainstream media reports about my misconduct with a patient, or two, would likely surface shortly. Turns out *three* have now made statements. I expect social media might be somewhat tougher on a shrink who likely has misbehaved.

"Arthur, this is terrible!" My old friend, from way-back-when, was unsettled, "Please, tell me it's not true." Randy smacked his lips and whistled a low sigh.

"Sorry, mate, but it happens." I couldn't lie, and Randy was an old ally.

"Did Dr. Quan suggest behavioural issues with the diagnosis?" Randy asked trying to make sense of my bombshell. "Did he call the psychology license board?"

"No, behaviour and brain malfunctions are likely correlated, but Dr. Quan is not prepared to travel down that road." No medical free pass for me on this one.

Randy grew more perplexed, "How did the licensing board and media find out about this?"

I smiled, shook my head, and said, "The police called them."

"The *police are involved?"*

"Afraid so," I took a drink. "Seems likely there will be some civil and criminal proceedings coming up."

"You got a lawyer, right?"

"Of course, I retained Craig Burris, QC, he's the best for these things."

Clearly, Randy was struggled trying to process this information. So, I thought I should say something to make my old pal smile and think of happy days. "Remember when you and Harjit came to visit me in Waikiki? We went surfing the big waves. That was some fun, eh?"

Randy's eyes were watery, "Yes, Artie, that was a tonne of fun."

Old Friends

Oh, how I love my old friends
The ones who knew me
From way back when
The ones who took me
Just as I am, old friends.

Do you remember we were climbing some steep hills?
Going for broke, searching out some cheap thrills.
We were drinking whiskey and some wine
Having such a good time
With my old friends.

Oh, don't the time slide by so fast
We put the pedal to the metal
Turned the music up full blast
We were singing, dancing,
Sometimes a little romancing
With my old friends.

All those miles we put behind us
Some familiar smiles to remind us
Of the good times, some songs
And we're still rolling along
With my old friends.

Oh, how I love
All of my old friends.

Hassles and a Husband

"What we see depends mainly on what we look for."
~John Lubbock (1834 – 1913)

Today my husband, Randal, leaves me a cryptic message on my chambers office voicemail, "Hi Harjit, I know you are in court this morning, but I wanted to leave you a message, so you'll know what's going on. Remember, I told you that Shane's in a coma. Well, now I must go to India to explain the situation to my niece, Amelia. It would be terrific if you could come with me. However, if my memory serves, I believe you mentioned that you are hearing a complicated case for the next few weeks. Okay, let me know, I've started making travel arrangements, first-class flying."

Although Randal has been out sorts lately since his old friend, Dr. Arthur Sutherland, has been formally charged with conduct unbecoming a psychologist, I am perplexed with Randal's recent pronouncement to travel *solo* to India. Last year when we went to India, he was overwhelmed most of the time. Unfortunately, shortly after we arrived, he ate some sort of roadside meat samosa and was ill for a few days. Nevertheless, he always seems to operate under the auspices of the positive pronoid professor effect. It's often been difficult to suggest maybe he cannot do something once he has decided he can. What could go wrong?

Additionally, since Arthur Sutherland disclosed his dementia diagnosis, Randal now seems to continually second-guess his own cognitive capabilities. If he has told me once, he has told me a hundred times, the B.F. Skinner story where Skinner says he knew his cognitive abilities were diminishing with age, but his wisdom was increasing. Randal is convinced *his* cognitive capabilities are diminishing; yet he wonders where his wisdom might reside.

Historically, Randal's always had splinter skill memory ability with names, dates and events. He never ceases to amaze me with his irregular memory skills. We'll be watching season six of some television series and Randal will say, "That's Bryan from season one." Myself, I hardly recognize the character, but Randal remembers the bloke's name and character details. Moreover, he is usually correct. A long-term splinter skilled memory marvel.

He has his strong points; just the same, for the life of me, Randal's never been any good putting *anything* together. IKEA, nothing but a nightmare. I'm oh so glad those days are long gone. We hire out nowadays. Money for that stuff is not an issue anymore. We've been working, saving and such.

And then the other day the whole door-key thing happened. It wasn't really a new issue, but for some reason or another Randal accelerated it into something bigger than it was after he learned about Arthur's diagnosis.

"*Fuckin' shit mother sucker*!" Randal shrieked at the locked door.

I'm standing behind him waiting for him to open the door. "What's happening?" I didn't know what he was on about. My hands were full of grocery bags. Even so, when he turned to face me, his expression was not favourable. "Randal, what's wrong?" I put my bags down on the garage's dirty concrete floor.

"Can't get the fucking key to work!" He said with exasperation.

"Randal don't worry about it. Here, I've got it." I simply put his key into the lock and opened the door. He got all uptight with distorted thoughts about his cognitive competence. He's left-handed and often turns things counter to how it is supposed to go.

"I swear, Randal, you are getting all messed up in your own head with *Arthur's problems.* Stop it, you are okay, there's nothing wrong with you!" Randal keeps thinking he's got what Arthur's got, but he doesn't. I know that. Dementia is *not* contagious.

We went inside, started unpacking the groceries, and the next thing I know he has sauntered off into his home office. I go in to check on him, and, of course, he's on the Internet checking out senility and dementia symptoms—on two separate screens.

"Randal, honey, aren't you the guy who always says: When in doubt, check it out. Really, that's what you should do, right."

He looked up from the screens, nodded, and said, "Yes, good idea."

"Cognitive conditions aren't contagious," I declared. "You know that, right."

"Yes, of course, it's just all these coincidences are uncanny."

So, a couple days go by, I ask whether he has made an appointment with Dr. Roberts. "No, not yet," he held up a palm. "I have a lot going on right now."

"Okay," I smile; yet think to myself, "Wonder if he's procrastinating or what's the deal now?" But, for all of that, don't get me wrong; Randal is the most amazing man I've ever known.

We met some twenty-six years ago in the grocery store, of all places. There I was trying to select apples, ones without big bruises and dents, when he comes strolling up to me.

"Hi, how you doing?" He's got a big smile that beams at me.

I look at him, trying to figure out who he is, and whether I know him. Or is this a come on line? "Excuse me, have we met before?"

"Yes, of course, I'm Dr. Randal Reilly," he said assertively. "I used to live in the same apartment building as you. But then I got a job and moved out."

Guess I must have scowled or something because he gets all defensive and says, "Got a job, that's a joke, get it. Got a job, doing a Jeffersons, you know, moving on up."

Now I know a scowl has overtaken my face. "Doing a Jeffersons?" I asked. "What's that?"

"Yeah, you know, Jeffersons that was a television show from 1975 to 1985. George Jefferson was a prosperous African-American businessman who was moving on up from Queens to Manhattan."

The penny dropped for me, "Yes, I remember that show. Well Dr. Reilly, glad to hear you are moving on up."

"Thanks." He gave me another big smile.

I placed a couple more apples into my cart and pushed on. "Nice to see you again Randal, see you around." We went in different directions and, at the time, I didn't think twice. I pushed on to the dairy section.

The next day I was thinking about the grocery store encounter with Dr. Randal Reilly. He seemed pleasant, thought I should give him a call and ask if he'd like to join me for coffee. "It's just coffee," I told myself.

After some schedule reconfiguration, we agreed to meet the next day at three in the afternoon at the Jericho Street Café.

The coffee shop connection went well enough that when he subsequently telephoned and asked me to join him for brunch date I agreed. We met downtown at the Hotel Van Bistro.

Our conversation was interesting, but Randal's speech pattern and diction can be confusing. We were discussing a complicated political calamity when I thought I heard him say he was a *Scientologist.* I was surprised, and asked, "You are a Scientologist?"

He scoffed, and said, 'No, I was speaking as a *social scientist.* I know nothing about *scientology*! I am a psychology social scientist. I adhere to the Scientist—Practitioner model."

"Very well, then," I said with a conciliatory tone. "That is good to know." I wasn't courting a scientologist.

The rest is history. We've been together for a long time now. It's good; he's a wonderful man, some eccentricities and peculiarities, but oh so kind and considerate. I love him more than anything in the world.

Consequently, Randal's message that he plans to travel solo to India is surprising on one hand, yet not on the other. He's always got something brewing, and maybe that's why I love him. Hope his trip to India goes off without a hitch. If I had my druthers, he would wait until we could go *together*. However, he can't wait, I can't just up and leave the court's stakeholders stranded, and besides hot weather in India is on the horizon. I'm not fond of hot weather.

Bon voyage my dear, be safe.

Part Two

INDIA TRAVELS

"You can't cross the sea merely by
standing and staring at the water."

~Rabindranath Tagore (1861 – 1941) won
the Nobel Prize for Literature in 1913.

Going to New Delhi

"All great truths begin as blasphemies."
~George Bernard Shaw (1856 – 1950)

Nephew Ned drove me to the airport in his sister's fire engine red mighty Mini Cooper which he was '*car-sitting*' while Amelia is gone and living in India.

Turning down the tunes on the car's music system in order for us to converse, Ned pivots to me and states, "Mum says she thinks you are running away from your problems by taking this trip to India."

"She said that?"

"Yeah!"

"Well, first off, I don't have any problems. Second, I'm not running away from anything! I'm taking a vacation in conjunction with informing Amelia and Raj about Shane's situation."

Reaching into his pocket, "Wanna use my phone, you could call them?"

"You call her!"

Ned scoffed, "I would, but now mum says *no calling*, it's inappropriate because you are going to India *in-person* to deliver the news about Shane."

"What do you think?"

"About Shane, or you going to India?"

"Both."

"Oh, man, this thing with Shane sure *sucks*! So glad mum was able to get Shane transferred from the stupid Saskatchewan prison hospital to the Vancouver General Hospital. Wish we knew what to expect next. Nobody seems to know. They don't have a prognosis, diagnosis or plan that's worth crap."

"Yes, as I understand it, the experts are reporting that Shane could come out of the coma at any time, or he might stay this way for a while. They just don't know."

"Yeah, we're taking shifts around the clock to be with him. At first the hospital balked, but mum bullied them into legal submission. We're just not allowed to make too much noise, and theoretically only three visitors at a time."

"Oh, by the way, I like the video song you beamed to me."

"Yeah, *Old Friends*. Ned smiled, "Great tune, eh?"

"I like it loud."

Ned snorted, "Logan and I were singing it live in Shane's hospital room, when they shut us down."

"Electric or acoustic?"

"We were unplugged, no amplifiers, we were playing acoustic. Craig Spelliscy and Blaine McNamee from Rufus Guitars showed me how to run the cable cord patch recorder through my cell phone's bluetooth. I'm sure Shane was happy with the setup. If he knew what was going on. Logan was on standup bass, and I was chopping the old Martin guitar with the cool scratch plate. I certainly didn't think we were *too* loud."

"Logan brought a standup bass to the hospital?"

"No, I did." Ned smiled, "Logan rode his bike to the hospital to meet me."

"How's Logan doing?"

Ned shakes his head and flips his wrist, "Aw, you know, Logan is Logan, he's always got issues. Rich people are like that, but

Shane's situation has really thrown Logan for a loop. We think he might be spending a bit too much time visiting at the hospital."

"How's Logan's family?"

"Aw, they're always supportive. Logan gets a wide margin from everyone."

"Betcha Banny, his daughter, doesn't cut Logan any slack."

"Hah, yeah, true that!" Ned smiles, "Yes, that's for sure, Banny gives it to Logan all the time."

Logan Meyers is one of Ned's best friends from childhood. Logan and his wife, Wendy, have a four-year-old daughter named Banny. She is a bundle of joy, energy, and sweetness. They all live in a large house with Logan's recently retired multi-millionaire stockbroker entrepreneur father, Gerald Meyers. These days Gerald spends most of his time choralling.

Their daughter, Banny Orton Meyers, is named after Banerjee Kaur Malik, a suicide victim that the boys discovered oh so many years ago at Camp Byng. I was with them when it happened. I was supposed to be one their chaperones. We were at the Boy Scouts Spring Campout on the Sunshine Coast near Gibsons, British Columbia.

Shortly after we arrived at the scout's campsite, nephew Ned, and his friends, Logan Meyers, Shane Bighill, and Raj Gill went *exploring*. Of course, as boys will do, they pushed the limits and went *exploring* in a zone beyond the explained permitted territory. While there they stumbled upon Banerjee Malik and Harpreet Dhaliwal who had entered into a suicide pact.

When the boys arrived at the suicide scene, Banerjee was already dead, hanging from a tree limb, but Harpreet was still alive. His weight was more than the limb he selected could hold, it broke, and his semi-asphyxiated body fell to the ground. Ned and Raj began performing cardiopulmonary first aide and artificial respiration while Logan and Shane raced back to the main campsite for adult help.

Although Harpreet had suffered some massive brain damage, he didn't die. The boys' first aide responses had saved Harpreet's life. And so, began a lifelong camaraderie between the boys, Harpreet, and their parents. It was never easy from the beginning, yet they persisted and made many advances in Harpreet's new life.

Besides Harpreet's medical complexities, all four boys, and, eventually, myself, were diagnosed with Post Traumatic Stress Disorder (PTSD). It's been a complicated path that we travel, to say the least. Individual differences, treatment compliance, and symptom recognition have been ongoing issues, for years.

The four boys showed differing degrees of Adolescent PTSD, and the resulting consequences. At age twelve Shane seemed to suffer the most. He started demonstrating various behavioural problems at school, in the community, and at home. As a teenager he began drinking too much, smoking too much marihuana, and his temper had a short fuse. "Shane shows some behavioural problems," said the school's psychologist. "He needs some intensive therapy."

When Shane was twenty-two, he was charged with second-degree murder. It really was an unfortunate incident from the get-go. Shane was simply walking home late at night when he overheard a couple thugs uttering racial taunts towards an Asian couple. Of course, Shane being Shane, he had to get involved. He told the Asian couple to move along. "Just get out of here don't let those guys get to you. I'll handle them."

The Asian couple crossed the street and went on their way. Shane stood up to face the thugs. The one guy pulled a knife on Shane and threatened him. Shane grabbed the knife, disarmed the thug, and stabbed him repeatedly. Then Shane chased down the other assailant and stabbed him, too. The end result was Shane had *killed* the two racist thugs.

My sister Annette, and niece, Amelia, served as Shane's defence lawyers throughout a protracted court case. Certainly, I thought they demonstrated a good case for self-defence. Initially, Shane did not have a weapon. Declan Downes had pulled the knife on Shane. In self-defence, Shane disarmed Declan and stabbed him with Declan's own knife. Unfortunately, a CCTV video surfaced showing Shane running down Trent Mckinney, who was trying to escape. Shane stabbed Trent with the knife he had taken from Declan. Thus, the prosecution maintained second-degree murder was the charge.

When all was said, and done, Shane settled for a manslaughter conviction. He was sentenced to four years in a federal prison. Usually, a four-year sentence translates into thirty-two months served with *good behaviour.* Unfortunately, Shane got into some sort of a skirmish with a couple prison guards, which led to him head butting one and punching the other. This infraction added another year to his sentence.

Currently, Shane is comatose, in a hospital, with a dubious prognosis.

We arrived at the airport. Ned tried to insist on accompanying me to the check-in. "No, thanks Ned, just drop me off," I slugged his shoulder. "Airport parking is too much of a hassle. I'll be fine."

"You sure?"

"Ned," I smiled, "On the list of people to worry about, put my name on page five. I'm fine."

"Yeah, yeah, for sure," Ned nodded at me, "I believe you, but everyone else is worried about you."

"I'm fine, going to India is good."

"Yes," Ned got a little watery-eyed. "Lotta stuff going on these days. Give Raj two newgees for me, one for Amelia."

"Will do."

I bailed out of the car, grabbed my bags, and gave Ned a bear hug. A newgee is a dumb old historical silly thing we've done since too long ago. That's where you grab a clump of someone's hair and vigorously rub his or her scalp with love, of course.

I hate goodbyes.

Ned Says, "He'll Be Fine."

"Some people feel the rain, others just get wet."
~Bob Marley (1945 – 1981)

My sister, Amelia, moved to India to be with one of my best friends, Raj Gill. In fairly short order they ended up getting *married.* As I understand the situation, they *had* to get married because it's India, and that is how it goes, according to Raj. He should know. My sister has always rolled rocks, big ones, uphill. It's her nature. Nevertheless, they got married. My mum had a bird.

"Amelia is way too young for marriage!"

"Dunno mum," I tried to get some logical traction, "Amelia is *thirty-one* years old."

Amelia's India departure was sudden, the marriage was sudden, and she left lots of loose ends behind. However, I can't complain because she left me the fire engine red Mighty Mini Cooper to drive while she was away. And that's a loose end in my favour. This car is high tech. The Mini has built in microprocessors, bells, whistles and all sorts of stuff I still haven't figured out.

Unfortunately, Amelia had a little bit of a meltdown before leaving Vancouver. I mean we all felt terrible when Shane got put in jail, but Amelia took a spiral south over the whole thing. Her self-imposed guilty feelings were inconsolable. Amelia was one of the junior lawyers working on Shane's case. My mum ended up being the lead lawyer when the allstar lawyer, Jedd Talbot, suddenly died. I thought Amelia and mum seemed to be working well together, but it got awkward when mum made Shane take a plea deal settlement for manslaughter, even worse when he got sentenced to four years in jail.

Amelia thought it was a *justified* self-defence claim and Shane should not go to jail. Before leaving she told me, "I should have fought harder for the self-defence claim. I feel guilty that I acquiesced, and now look how it ended. Shane's in jail."

Of course, I told her not to be so self-centeredly dumb, "Amelia, don't take it so personally." Still, she did. Lawyering didn't work out. At least she also has a medical degree to fall back on. I think she'll be okay. It takes time. High strung people are like that. She's my only sister. She's always been difficult.

One of the coolest features this car has is the Bluetooth satellite calling application. I push the phone button on the steering wheel; speak into the dashboard, and say, "Call Nina." And ring-a-ling, ring-a-ling the call is made. Naturally, of course, I get Nina's voicemail because she never answers, never.

"Hi Nina, I'm leaving the airport now. Just dropped off Uncle R. He's on his way to India. He'll be fine. Okay, see you soon. I'm stopping to pick up ice cream at Dairy Queen."

Nina is Shane's fraternal twin sister. She's also my partner. We've been living together for over four years now, since Shane's incarceration. At first my mum had a conniption about it, but Uncle R helped her get through it. As a high-powered lawyer, my mum is legally competent but in her personal life, she catastrophes things when it comes to her kids. When I moved in with Nina my mum was convinced, she'd become a grandmother overnight. It hasn't happened yet, but it might. And that's not a bad thing, yet the overall timing might be a bit off. Nina is in charge.

Lately, sixty-three-year-old Uncle R has been having a tough time. He's convinced that his cognitive decline trajectory is too steep and he's heading for a crash. Really, it's not true, but trying to convince him of it is not easy. To make things worse his long-time buddy, Dr. Arthur Sutherland, got diagnosed with premorbid demented senility. Additionally, Arthur got into some legal difficulties when he was charged with sexual assaulting some of his patients. All this weighs heavy on Uncle R. I think that's why he decided to get outta Dodge and travel to India. Really, he could've just called Amelia about Shane's coma. Uncle R has been to India a few times before, he likes it there. Aunty Harjit's family are all exceptionally nice to Uncle R.

When Shane, Logan, Raj, and I found Banny. She was dead hanging from a tree. Harpreet lying on the ground, barely alive. Uncle R got us through it. We were kinda messed up. It was a terrible time. We were all diagnosed with Adolescent Post Traumatic Stress Disorder. Banny was diagnosed with being dead. Harpreet had hypoxic ischemic encephalopathy—brain damage due to oxygen deprivation, but he lived. We were all kinda screwed up, some of us more than others. Uncle R explains, "These things aren't linear. And it might take some time to get to the other side. There's no formula or magic pill for these things."

Uncle R got me through puberty. It was a confusing time, but it wasn't all that tough, all things considered, yet Uncle R got me through it. My body was changing, hormones raging, and my mind was something else altogether. Thankfully, I had Uncle R. It was always helpful to talk to him about the things my mum didn't understand about boys, sex drives, and what girls really wanted.

Although Uncle R's current cognitive decline is *not* analogous to my sojourn through puberty, some parallels and tangents are there from a socio-biological theoretical perspective. So, whatever, I am determined to help him get through it.

He'll be fine.

The Bro Knows Best

"There is no right way to do a wrong thing."
~Dr. Perry T. Leslie (1944 – 2017)

The best thing about my brother Raj—he has always helped me deal with our parents. I couldn't do it without him. Glad I'm not an only child trying to deal with the parents.

"Parmy, just grab onto my coattails. I'll clear a path for you," Raj says with a smile.

Thanks bro, you're the leader.

Most of the time our parents are reasonably tolerable, but every now and then they can both get quirky and a little nutty. Together, separately, or as a tag team duo they can drive me to check into the Port Coquitlam psych ward with their wrong way thoughts and projections. Sometimes I get sucked in way too easily. Raj is three years older, and he seldom has these difficulties. Mostly because Raj is male, he just walks away, and doesn't bother bickering with them. I *try* to reason with them. Logical analyses and reasonable thought processes are not always a reality with our parents.

Over the long distance telephone Internet line, Raj patiently explains, "Parmy, the folks are the folks, you cannot reason with them because they are the folks. Once you understand that fact, life with them will be a lot easier for you."

Oh sure, easy for him to say, when I'm the one trying to explain to the folks why I'll be arriving *three* days later than what I originally declared.

"Mummy, *mutta jee,*" I must explain in Punjabi, and then again in English, to try and get her hysteria dialed down. "I will arrive *three days* later. It's no big thing."

What happened was Raj told his friend, Ned Reilly, that I was flying to New Delhi to attend Chaachee auntie's end of life honouring ceremonies. So, Ned then tells Raj that *his* Uncle R is also flying to New Delhi, too. However, he is scheduled to leave *three* days after my scheduled departure date. The next thing I know is those two are plotting to get me travel to Delhi with Uncle R as his travel *guide.*

I'd already booked my ticket, plans were set in place, and I was reluctant to change, but it was Raj asking. It is hard for me to say no thanks to him. Besides, he was sweetening the pot. "I will upgrade your ticket to *First Class*!" he says.

"Raj," I scoff, "Nowadays there's no such thing as pompous *First Class* anymore. It's called *Business* travel. For such a smart guy you are sometimes so *dumb.*"

"First Class, Business Class there is no difference."

I scoffed at him. "Other than elitist lingo, right Raj." I said with a laugh. "Steerage sounds low class, while *economy* not so pejorative, eh?"

"Whatever, Ned and I need you to help here," he sighed. "Okay."

"Yes, Raj, you got it, of course, I'll do it."

"Thanks, Parm, you're the best sister ever. You'll see when you open your email that I've already sent you an upgraded e-ticket. You are sitting in the pod-seat across from Uncle R."

"*He's not your uncle, Raj!*" I said, a little more forcefully than likely needed.

"Hey, Parm, listen, Ned says Uncle R is going through a rough patch these days. He is not as crisp as he once was, and he feels bad about it. Something is going on with the guy."

"Okay."

"And Parm," Raj seems to choke and his voice croaks. "Uncle R is very important to me. I'd do anything for him. *Anything*."

"Okay, okay, yes, Raj, I won't let you down." I added, "You can count on me."

Brotherly commitments and family obligations, yikes.

Flying still mesmerizes me. The idea that this giant metal airplane tube thing gets off the ground and travels thousands of miles is amazing. The physics, the math, and the fact that it happens are still overwhelmingly for me to think about. I love flying. However, I hate being sedentary, buckled in a seat, for twenty hours straight. That just sucks.

This will be my fourth trip to India. The first two count because truthfully, I did indeed travel to India with my family, but I don't remember much, I was too little. The third trip was terrible. The flight took *forever*. I was thirteen years old and antsy. Sitting still for boring hour after hour was torture. At first, I had to sit by my brother, then they made me sit with my mother. I fell asleep for a while, but what I remember most was the unending torture of flying.

So, this time, when Raj paid to bump me up from cheapskate's steerage Economy Class to a luxury pod in Business Class travel, I was relieved and slightly thrilled. Now, the true thing is, I have money. I don't have as much money as my brother, but my bank account is fluid. I've saved up some cash over time. I'm certainly solvent. Trouble is I cannot lie to my father. He'd have a coronary if he found out that I blew a wad of dough on *Business Class* luxury travel. "What a *waste of money*," Pops would moan. Yet, if my brother, Rajinder, was to waste money by buying me a bumped-up ticket, Pops could cope with that. "It is proper for Rajinder to take care of his sister. That is his *duty.*"

My family is BIG on duty, traditions, and responsibilities. Although some of this stuff represents long-standing life-struggles for me, I go along to get along. The long road, the high road, and family dynamics are all matters that mean more than my energy can handle. Raj says, "Pick your battles, carefully." Yeah, he should know. He got that from Charles de Gaulle. Raj has had more than one classic Pyrrhic victory with Pops.

In the old days, my parents would fly back home to India leaving from Vancouver to Toronto, change planes. Then they would fly from Ontario to England, change planes, and finally fly to New Delhi. Now that was a long trip. No way would I do that type of travel. I'd rather just stay home. I don't need to go anywhere that badly.

Anyhow, the big bonus with this current flight is we are travelling via the *polar route,* which takes hours off the old route's flying time. This is *only* a fifteen-hour flight. Last time our family flew the North Pacific Ocean route. That flight leaves Vancouver and goes over the Pacific Ocean, eventually ending in Delhi. This polar route flight is way shorter by going over the North Pole. We will fly direct, but with a few jigs and jags around countries like Pakistan, Afghanistan and other Stans where their airspace is prohibited. This is as good as it's going to get.

I started thinking about the young American couple that was murdered in Tajikistan. I can't remember their names, but they had left high-power finance jobs to go cycling around the world. They had covered a lot of territory on their bicycles before Tajikistan. There a group from ISIS mowed them down with their Daewoo sedan. Dashboard video was hard to unwatch. They were murdered.

Finally, I got through security without too much hassle. I'm brown skinned, so it's always a crapshoot at airport screening. After that I made my way through the labyrinth of the airport's passageways. And, because of my *business* class status, I was one of the first to board the airplane. A handsome flight attendant escorted me to my seat/pod. It was awesome! "Would you like some champagne?"

I immediately texted pics of my seating pod to Kelsey Pearce and Edilma Calderón. "Thanks for driving me to the airport." Caitlyn Chan couldn't come because she had an *important* boyfriend rendezvous. Otherwise, she would have done the bon voyage farewell mission too, I think. The four of us have been best of friends since first Year University—which seems like forever ago now.

Kelsey got me through Organic Chemistry. It was tough stuff to try and learn, but Kelsey got me to think about Organic Chem in terms of a Tetris puzzle. That was all I needed, someone to reframe it. We worked our way through the assignments and studied together. I made it through the course—got a final grade of 82%, which is an acceptable grade of 'B'. Whew.

I'm still fairly sure that Caitlyn wasn't purposely dodging me, yet I don't know, deep down, because last week we went a little weird with things. For sure, Caitlyn shouldn't drink tequila, she can't handle hard alcohol. Her face gets all red and flushed. Edilma explains that Caitlyn has the Asian bio-chemical reaction where the hemoglobin and oxygen are saturated and produce a chemical reaction. "The protein enzymes and substrates show an inability for complete synthesis. They can't metabolize easily. Similarly, when the Canadian First Nations Indigenous people were fur trading for alcohol. They called it *firewater.* It really was like firewater because of their bio-chemical reaction. The Irish and Scots have been drinking whiskey for centuries. Genetically speaking, they are conditioned. Alcohol was a new thing for the Canadian Indigenous peoples. It didn't work out well for the Irish either." Edilma is an expert on this stuff.

"Edilma, how do you know this stuff?"

"It's science," she responded with a smirk and a clenched fist in the air.

Whatever, I don't know, maybe we shouldn't have started drinking the stupid sparkling wine. Whose idea was that?

So, Caitlyn says, "Parm, you want to go upstairs with me to pee and powder?"

"Sure, good idea. All this booze is flowing through me."

So, there we were in the upstairs master bathroom peeing, hair brushing, and doing beauty work. We were quite wasted, when suddenly Caitlyn leans over and kisses me. She kissed me hard and passionately. It was my first gay kiss. I didn't know what to think. So, when she started fondling my breast, I grabbed hers, too. Then she bit my neck with a little nibble. She stuck her tongue in my ear. But then, suddenly, her boyfriend, Joel, comes out of nowhere and starts pounding loudly on the bathroom door yelling, "Caitlyn, you in there. I've been looking all over for you."

She looked at me, I looked at her, we straightened ourselves up, opened the door, and I slipped past Joel. "See you later kids," I said, "gotta go check on Kelsey. She's driving me home."

We haven't spoken about it, yet. I'm sure we will, we *have* to, I think. Actually, I don't know what to think. The whole sex thing is complicated. Edilma's friend, Louise Davis, claims she is a bi-sexual, pansexual person. Of course, Kelsey couldn't listen and just leave it alone. She had to ask, "What does that mean?"

"It means I like sex, in great quantities and high quality," Louise replied. "Men generally are into quantity sex, while women are good quality sex."

"Okay, good to know," I said, nodding an acknowledgement. "The old quality versus quantity love story."

Historically, for me, the thing is, *everyone* knows more about sex than I do. Of course, over the past few years, I've had sex, like a dozen times with *three* different guys. And it was fine, it was okay, I mean the earth didn't shake or anything, but I am quite sure that I am heterosexual.

I had a boyfriend, for a while, well sort of a boyfriend. It was only for a few months and in the end, it turned out I was sharing Wes Roberts with a couple other cuckolds.

With some French white wine, Kelsey helped me wallow through to the other side of contentment. She used the lots of other fish in the sea scenario and stuff like that. I was feeling low, so Kelsey pulled out the stops and pulled me through to the other side of understanding what Wes was about. "Some men are like that."

Edilma, on the other hand, her people are from Puerto Rico, she said, "We should go over there and cut his nuts off."

Kelsey made an unhappy noise, gave Edilma a glare. "Not helpful right now Eddie. Thanks just the same."

Of course, my protected childhood hasn't helped either. At any rate, after my encounter with Caitlyn, now I'm wondering about Louise's bisexual pansexual stuff. Maybe I'm missing something?

Caitlyn Chan doesn't care. She is so bold. She is always out there doing this and that with no concerns. I was born in Canada, but in terms of acculturation, I am behind. Caitlyn's people built the Canadian Pacific Railroad. She is like fourth generation Canadian Chinese. She looks Chinese, yet for some reason she proudly claims that she can't speak a word of Chinese. English is my third language. I spoke Punjabi and Hindi for the first six years of my life, and then I had to go to school. English is kind of a weird language, certainly different from Punjabi and Hindi.

I asked my mother, “Why didn’t you send me to Kindergarten?”

“We didn’t have to,” she shrugs, “so we didn’t.”

Consequently, when I showed up in the first grade at Kitsilano Elementary School, I had to learn English quickly. I had no choice. English wasn’t so hard to learn. The culture was another matter altogether. Thank goodness I had my big bro Raj to help. I am so looking forward to seeing him. I’ve missed him.

I was deep into my thoughts about the past, present and possible future, wondering whether I did *something* to sexually lead Caitlyn on, but, if so, it was unconscious on my part. Then I realized someone was speaking to me, gesturing and saying, “You-who.” Took a couple of seconds, and I shook out of my daze.

“Namastè,” it was Uncle R, calling and waving to me from the seat/pod across the aisle.

“Hi,” I waved back to him. “Great seats, eh? Business class is the *best* way to travel.”

He gave me a wry smile with a wink and said, “Yes, it’s the *only* way to fly to India.”

So, okay, here we go, flying to India for *fifteen* hours.

“It’ll be fine,” I whisper to myself.

Part Three

SHANE BIGHILL

"Finding a key on the ground is useless until you know which door to unlock."

~Dr. Ronald F. Jarman (1941 – 1995)

Mind and Brain – Behaviours

"Today is only one day in all the days that will ever be. But what will happen in all the other days that ever come can depend on what you do today."
~Ernest Hemingway (1899 – 1961) wrote in F*or Whom the Bell Toll*s.

"Hello, Shane Bighill, are you awake?" asked the white angel at the end of my bed.

"Yes, guess so." I answered with trepidation.

"You have been in a coma." She seemed excited. "I'll be back in a moment. I have to call Dr. Sidhu."

"Okay."

I could hear her in the hallway calling out, "Tell Dr. Sidhu that Nurse Donnelly must speak with him straightaway."

I could hear noises and excited voices. This can't be a good thing.

~

Wonder what kind of coma I've been in?

Some things come back to me sorta, but not really. Mostly I'm malingering something, yet I don't know what.

~

Now the angel is saying I was back to life, but then I relapsed back down again, "What do you remember?"

I do remember being in jail or maybe I was too involved with some weird video game. "Am I still in a coma now?" I asked.

She nodded her head, "Yes," was all she said. So, I shouldn't argue.

The white angel walked away, and then I was all alone. So, this is a coma, but maybe it's a dream.

Now when I think about it, can't conceive just how extraordinarily weird it was that a video camera that got me put in jail, and now it's a video cam that is going to get me out.

When we were in court facing my murder charges the crown prosecution people showed everyone the CCTV video of me killing Declan Downes. It didn't look good. Wish I hadn't done that. Also, the crown prosecutor reported that they have found an independent witness who says I chased Trent McKinney, threw him to the ground, and stabbed him to death. That was off camera, but Ned says, "Legally, that'd be a double whammie, the CCTV video *and* witness evidence could not be refuted." Well, whatever, it was the truth. I did do it. I killed those two guys. Of course, if I could go back in time, I'd do things differently. Such is the way these things work. No time travelling.

Ned's mum was my main lawyer. She did a plea bargain deal to get the charges pulled down from second-degree murder to manslaughter. Ned and everyone else in the courtroom screamed that it was *self-defence,* and I should go free. Judge Wallace didn't see the facts that way. I got sentenced to four years in a federal penitentiary.

At first, they sent me to the federal penitentiary in the Fraser Valley just outside of Abbotsford. It wasn't great, it was a prison, but it was okay because my friends could come and visit. Then I got in a kerfuffle with a couple of guards. One had spit in my food because I called him an asshole. The other didn't care until I head butted the shithead guard. Then all hell broke loose. After that, I got sent to a prison in Saskatchewan with another year added to my sentence. There goes the *good behaviour* prison scam. I'm no one's suckhole.

Thinking backwards this business about the mind versus the brain thing was first explained to me when I was around thirteen years old. Those teenage years were tough. These days I'm still figuring it all out. But back when we were thirteen, Logan Meyers and I saw the same shrink together for a while. Dr. Shelley Dickie was nice. We had never heard about *suicide pacts,* until we discovered the pact with Banny and Harpreet. Dr. D explained how some of those pact things worked. Yet nobody knows really what they were thinking. Nothing is as simple as it seems.

For sure, Logan was weird and uptight before we got the Adolescent PTSD diagnosis, but then he was way worse afterwards. Mind you, Logan says the same about me, too. I don't know. Ned and Raj seemed okay with the dead girl, but it turned out they had their own issues.

Thank Zeus, Buddha, and all the other gods for my friends. They're the ones that get me through the tough stuff. Don't know what life would be like without them.

Dr. Shelley D explained that most of my problems were with my mind. My brain was fine. Logan and I learned that information processing was a brain thing. Thinking was the mind matter. I had some thought disorders, misconceptions, and intrusive thinking problems. However, I wasn't completely schizoid or anything, but I could misinterpret things the wrong way, and that was sometimes problematic. Sometimes I got into trouble unnecessarily.

Right now, in this hospital bed, I know it's my brain that is in trouble. Don't know how long it took me to figure things out. I distinctly remember the Saskatchewan prison, the smell and sounds. I remember the guard smashing my head on the floor. Yet after that most of my memory is fuzzy.

Stretched out horizontally on this hospital bed I can hear stuff going on around me, but I can't speak. I can't move neither. Guess that means I'm paralyzed. Too bad I am the only one who knows that this thinking and brain malfunction is the deal. It is an organic fact. My mind is working, however, my brain can't send signals, speak, or let anyone know I am still here. They've put monitoring machines on me, poked me with pins, and I hear them say "they're running tests." Whatever, I'm still here, sort of, but not really. Nobody likes needles, tubes and IV drips.

A nice lady, who turned out to be a physiotherapist, comes in the room and works on my body. When she leaves a nurse comes in and gives me needles. I've always hated needles, yet no way could I flinch or refuse the needle.

My friends are here at the hospital all the time visiting. Nurses and doctors come around to suggest the gang keep the noise down. They are always saying, "Please don't touch the monitors or equipment, okay."

Nobody tells Logan what to do.

Ned's mum comes at nighttime, holds my hand, and cries. Wish I could tell her that it's okay. I'll wake up and come out of this coma, when the time is right. "It's okay Mrs. Reilly, don't cry for me."

I really like it when Logan brings his four-year-old daughter, Banny, to visit. She is so sweet. While Logan and Ned were engrossed singing some new songs; Banny climbed on top of me and opened my eyelids. It was good. I could see! I started blinking, it seemed like Banny understood what I was saying through eye blinks. "Daddy, daddy, look, Uncle Shane is saying something."

Logan and Ned just kept on keeping on because keeping time musically was their thing. Ned's bio dad is a real musician and Logan's bio mum is a violinist with the Seattle Symphony. Don't talk to those guys about genetics; it's not worth the discussion. Music is relative, especially for those two.

Just when the boys were singing the second chorus, my twin sister, Nina, and Wendy, who is Logan's common law wife, burst into the room carrying a load of shopping parcels. Wendy dropped her bags on the floor, "Logan, don't let Banny climb all over Shane," Wendy shrieked pointing the index finger of doom. She dashed over and scooped Banny off me, "Darling, don't touch Uncle Shane's eyes, okay."

"But he was blinking signals to me," Banny tried to explain.

"Really," Wendy said with a skeptic's nodding head.

"Yes, he was," Banny said.

Oh, how I wanted to say, "Yes, Banny is telling the truth. I was sending her a message."

Now I know how Harpreet must have felt when he was in the hospital all those years ago. Took a while before the officials and parental units would let us see Harpreet in the hospital. Permission was withheld because back then we were only twelve years old. Our parents, his parents, and most of the doctors all thought we were too young to understand the situation. Yeah, no shit, took a long time to understand.

Harpreet and I became best of friends. His brain was damaged badly from the suicide attempt, but his mind was okay. And that's what's going on with me now. My brain got rattled and smashed by the prison guards. My mind is working, I'm thinking things, but just like Harpreet I can't talk. So, nobody knows it 'cept me, right now. And four-year-old Banny.

Ned came to visit me in the hospital late at night. I can tell the difference between night and day in the hospital because the sounds are different, important people are only here during the day, and the rhythms are different. Ned was all excited, worked up, and was telling me that his mum had got some sort of a subpoena for prison CCTV video. That video shows the Saskatchewan guards beating on me and smashing my head on the concrete floor. Now the court has agreed that when I come out of the coma, I will be set free. Too bad because I'm in a coma-type prison now. And in many ways, it is worse than Saskatchewan.

"So come on Shane," Ned coaxed. "You gotta wake up. You gotta come out of this coma. Okay."

I would if I could.

Fraternal Twins

"We can complain because rose bushes have thorns or
rejoice because thorn bushes have roses."
~Abraham Lincoln (1809 – 1865)

My brother Shane and I are fraternal twins. I was born first; Shane made his grand entrance eight minutes later. As fraternal twins we share a lot of the nature/nurture history. However, truth be told, we are so dissimilar in so many, many ways. Dad always reminded me, "Nina, you *are* the oldest." That was dad's default line.

Today, at age twenty-eight, Shane has already seen some tough stuff. He's had too many critical incidents to count. Yet, deep down, I've always known there was more to come. He was just getting stated when we were kids.

When Shane was eleven or twelve, I can't remember exactly, he and his friends went camping with the Boy Scouts. There they stumbled on a suicide pact, which forever changed several lives. The girl died, but Shane and his friends saved the guy's life. His ligature or branch broke. At any rate, the boys saved him. His name is Harpreet. He had massive brain damage due to the suicide attempt. Shane and his friends became best of friends with Harpreet. They looked after him, helped Harpreet's rehabilitation, and enriched his life. Of course, they say Harpreet has enriched their lives just as much, if not *more*.

After the suicide pact discovery, Shane was diagnosed with Adolescent Post Traumatic Stress Disorder. He obsessed and dwelled on the girl's death, thinking if they had only been there sooner, they could have saved Banny's life, too. Shane's behaviour at home and school deteriorated. He seemed to always be getting into trouble. If it wasn't one thing it was another. He developed a quick temper, got into fights for little or no reason, caused all sorts of trouble, and became a burden for our parents.

Hard to believe, but things got a lot worse when we were eighteen years old. Our parents were killed in a car crash. They were on their way to a family function in Kelowna. A young woman driving a pickup truck down the mountain highway along Westport Road to the Fintry Estate Parkway lost control of her truck, crossed the centre line, and hit my parent's car head on.

I'll always remember, at the time, I was in a laboratory tutorial at UBC, two RCMP officers came through the back door, spoke to the Lab Teaching Assistant, Jenny Ponsort. She pointed to our lab station. Jokingly, I said to my lab partner, "Uh oh, Susan, cops coming for you."

Turns out it wasn't all that funny after all. The older male officer approached us, "Hello, are you Ms. Nina Bighill?"

"Yes," I was sort of surprised and wondered, "What did Shane do now?"

The woman RCMP officer touched me on the elbow and softly asked, "Maybe we could go out in the hallway to speak for a moment?"

"Okay."

Out in the hallway I asked, "What's going on?"

The older male officer took off his hat, "I am sorry to tell you Ms. Bighill that your parents have been involved in a serious car accident today."

I gasped, "What?" I was expecting to hear about something Shane had done. Certainly, wasn't expecting to hear my parents were *dead.*

The police were sensitive, given the circumstances, yet I was overwhelmed with the whole thing. They drove me to the

Vancouver General Hospital Morgue where we waited for my parents' bodies to be delivered. I was there for formal identification purposes.

Andrea, the female police officer, who had brought me to the hospital, came walking over with another woman. "Hi Nina, this is Peggy Zimmerman from the Kelowna Fire Department."

Peggy stuck out her perspiring warm hand, we shook hands firmly, and she said, "Mind if I sit with you a moment?"

Okay, what am I supposed say, everyone likes firefighters, but I'm a little stressed right now? Whatever, "Sure, have a seat." I motioned with a wave of my hand to the seat beside me.

Peggy lightly touched me on the knee, and spoke softly, "I promised your father that I would talk to you."

"Okay." Now she had my attention. "You spoke with my dad?"

She grimaced, "Yes, we were the first responders to the accident scene. Unfortunately, your mother had already passed from her injuries. Your father was still conscious when I got there. I talked to him; trying to reassure that we were going to do everything we could to help him. We used the Jaws of Life machine to get him out of the car successfully. But shortly after we got him out of the car, he succumbed to his injuries. His last words to me were to tell Nina that she was in charge now. He wanted me to tell you that it's up to you to look after Shane now.

Peggy pointed over to the cops, "The RCMP have told me that Shane is your brother."

I nodded. "Yes, that's correct." Tears were rolling down my face. I was sniffling and losing all control.

Andrea came over and handed me a tissue, "Would you like us to come with you to explain what happened to your brother, Shane?"

"No, that's fine thanks," I shook my head. "It's something I'd rather do by myself." I started to regain composure, I reassured them that dealing with Shane was best accomplished by me as a soloist. And, as Peggy the firefighter said, dad delegated taking care of Shane. It was now my responsibility.

I tracked Shane down at Logan Meyers' house. They were heavily involved in some sort of an online video game tournament, and Shane was reluctant to come home. I think he could tell from the tone of my voice that something had happened and negotiating with me was not a good idea. "Logan's killing a guy from Kansas, but okay, fine, whatever you want Nina. I'll be home in a minute."

Herding cats and looking after my brother were much the same. We had some good times, and tough times, too. Shane drank too much, smoked too much weed, and got into too many fights. He was charming, yet obstinate, and if it wasn't for his friends, I think things would have been more difficult. He had, still has great friends.

When Shane was twenty-three, life hit a brick wall. He killed two young men during an altercation in Vancouver's Yaletown district. Evidentially, the two men had thrown racial slurs at an Asian couple that was walking down the street in front of Shane. He took exception to their taunts. One guy pulled a knife and waved it at Shane. Never a good idea to taunt Shane. He somehow disarmed the guy with the knife and stabbed him to death. The other guy tried to run away. Shane chased him down and killed him, too. CCTV caught it all on camera. The video became evidence during his trial. An eyewitness testified; he saw Shane kill the two young men.

After a long-drawn-out trial, Shane was convicted of manslaughter and sentenced to four years in federal prison. The trial had been a protracted ordeal for everyone. There were many twists and turns all along the way. We were always hoping for the best, but I always expected the worst. In the end they put him in handcuffs, dragged him out of the courtroom, and carted him off to jail. It was a sad situation for all of us, especially Shane.

The same day Shane was incarcerated Ned, my boyfriend, and Shane's best friend from childhood, showed up at my place and announced, "I'm moving in." He had two carloads of his *stuff.* Logan helped with unloading the boxes, bags, and instruments from his car. Logan motioned a faux hello to me, but he couldn't talk, or say anything sensible.

Ned said, "Don't mind him, he's in a mood."

I was in a mood, too. Nevertheless, I was happy to see those two shuffling around, moving things to accommodate Ned's prized possessions. That was five years ago now. Time might travel in a linear line, but life does not.

I had been working late in the lab, I was dead tired, but thought I should visit Shane in the hospital before going home. He's been in a coma for over a month now. The *experts* do not agree on etiology or prognosis. "He could come out of the coma tomorrow," says the hipster resident lab coat guy. The older physician shakes his head, "Yes, that is true, although I should say, Shane may never come out of the coma. We do not know for certain, at this point."

Ned and the guys had setup a vigil. When Shane was first transferred from the Saskatchewan prison hospital to Vancouver General Hospital, they guys were by his side 24/7. They talk to Shane is if he could hear. They sing songs, although hospital staff have asked, if they could *please* keep noise down to a reasonable decibel level. They don't. They've always been a noise bunch, Shane and his friends.

Tonight, when I got there, Shane's eyes were *open*, but non-responsive. Ned's eyes were closed. He was sound asleep. Ned had climbed up on the bed to lie beside Shane.

I started to cry, don't really know why, other than this is so emotional. I love those two more than anything. Rather than waking Ned and taking him home, I just sat down in the chair by the bed.

Guess I fell asleep in the chair. Around six in the morning four-year-old Banny Meyers came trotting into the hospital room, "Hi everyone, we're here. Daddy's down the hall peeing. And I'm supposed to let Daddy pee in private when we are outside of our house. Mummy says so."

Ned woke up, "Good morning Banny, what time is it?"

"Dunno, ask daddy," she said while climbing up on the bed.

"Mummy's home sleeping so we are here!"

Ned smiled, blew me a kiss, and gave Banny a big hug.

After a moment or two Logan saunters into the hospital room.

"Alright, it's party time."

Amelia's Angst

"The road to success is always under construction."
~Lily Tomlin

Before the murder trial I never really *knew* Shane all that well. I knew Shane had been with my brother and uncle when they stumbled upon the suicide pact all those years ago. I knew that he and Nina are fraternal twins. I knew that their parents were killed in a car crash. So, sure, I knew a lot *about* Shane. He had been hanging around our house for years, but during the murder trial I really got to know him. I had a good understanding of what he was all about.

I understood the overall gestalt of the murder. Now, knowing Shane, I knew why he did it. How it happened made sense to me. Clearly, to my way of thinking, it was self-defence, all the way. No ifs or ands or buts about it. *Automaticity* instincts kicked in and that's what happened. Shane reacted, maybe it was impulsive, but it made sense to me. I understood how it happened.

So, of course, I took it personally when Shane was convicted of manslaughter. The trial process had dragged on too long. In the end it was a plea bargain deal from second-degree murder reduced to manslaughter. My mother negotiated the out-of-court settlement. Even though she *agreed* with my insistence that self-defence was correct, she wouldn't take it to trial. Shane's previous criminal infractions, although minor, seemed to be relevant. The CCTV video evidence and eyewitness testimony seemed to convince her that we'd lose in a trial. Shane would be convicted of second-degree murder.

I, on the other hand, was certain a jury would see the situation as self-defence. All we had to do was present a convincing self-defence case. The jury would understand. But my mother wouldn't do it. She made like it was Shane's choice, to accept or reject the plea bargain, but there was more pressure than I thought necessary. In the end Shane took the plea deal and was sentenced to four years in federal prison.

I was completely beside myself. Sequentially and successively, I felt sad, mad, and bad. It just wasn't the eventual outcome we expected and wasn't warranted. Although Shane was going to jail, I took it too personally. This was wrong. Shortly, sometime afterwards, was when I quit talking to my mother.

Just to escape from all the unhappiness, I took off for India to be with my boyfriend, Raj. It was my first trip to India; I only lasted a little over two weeks. I just couldn't cope with all the customs, rules—written and unwritten, and all the *noise*. Raj tried to tell me all the honking of horns was a type of courtesy. An Indian custom. "When the horn is honked it is polite to let the other car know you are coming through." Whether it was true or not, it was too much for me.

To get around town, Raj rode a funky motorbike. I liked it. However, when he said I should cover my head and face with a scarf while we ride around town, I let him have it. I got angry. Maybe, I overreacted, a bit, but it was one of those things that was hard to tolerate. "That's a *stupid* custom!"

Raj was innocent, he didn't understand, "Amelia, why are you so angry? All the women cover their head and face because of the dust. And, besides that, anonymity is important so nosy ones will not know who is riding behind the man. You know, maybe the wrong type of woman could be riding on the back of the bike."

"What?" I couldn't believe what I was hearing. "That's the stupidest thing I've ever heard!"

I couldn't cope with all the unwritten rules. Then I was just so sad, mad, and feeling bad about everything. So, I decided to go back home. Turns out that was even more of a mistake. I became even more miserable once I got home. I was alone and without my best friend, Raj.

I waited for the right time of day, morning, and I called Raj. I apologized and asked if I could return. Maybe we could live to together. You know, a fairytale ending: *Amelia and Raj lived happily ever after.*

"We would have to be married to live together in India," Raj tried to be tactful.

"Really."

"Yes, that's how it works here. We would need to be married."

So, okay, that wasn't quite the storybook romantic marriage proposal I would have preferred; yet I agreed. "Fine, let's get married. I love you, Raj. We should be together."

"I love you, too!" Raj sighed.

Then I realized I must emphasize, "No fancy elaborate Indian ceremonies, either." In India wedding ceremonies are big events running over a week or so. Besides, Raj's uncle has been shopping him around for an *arranged marriage.* Raj is a good catch; everyone knows that.

"If you don't want to have a marriage ceremony in India, I could fly back to Vancouver," Raj cajoled. "We could get married at City Hall or the church of your choice."

Although I knew my father would be absolutely delighted to *walk me down the aisle,* I am still not speaking to my mother. So, no, we're not traveling that route.

"UBC's Museum of Anthropology?" Raj wasn't giving up easily. "We could have a civil ceremony amongst the Haida totem poles. Judge Angelomatis could officiate."

"I don't know," I moaned with a tone of exasperation.

"Yeah, yeah, it would be good. My sister's friend, Kelsey Pearce is a museum docent. We could use the Museum of Anthropology great hall overlooking the ocean."

The thing was, I didn't want a lot of fancy fuss, pomp and ceremony. I just wanted to be with Raj. I just want to live with Raj. However, Raj insisted that life in India, and our relationships at the University of Punjab would be much, much easier if we married. So, fine, I agreed to marry. Life is too short for unnecessary hassles.

In the end, after many back and forth discussions, Raj flew back to Vancouver. We had a small private ceremony on my uncle's cottage deck overlooking the Salish Sea on Mayne Island. And that was that, we were married. Raj was happy, and we could live together in India without his father and various busybodies hassling him. I didn't feel any different, but Raj did. I guess he just felt being married made him legitimate. Raj doesn't like conflict; he doesn't like it when his family is disappointed with him. Me, I couldn't care less. I'm not sweating small stuff.

These days, Raj keeps leaving little family crumbs around our house with the hope I will respond to my mother's never-ending barrage of messages—voicemail, email, and texts. Of course, I already know about Shane's coma. We have the Internet, I read the news reports, I don't need my mother to tell me what has happened. It's mainstream media headline news. Social media exploded with Shane's situation. Sure, I'm living in India, yet not cocooned in a vacuum. I know what's going on.

Now as I understand it, my Uncle Randal is traveling to India to tell me *in-person* about Shane's coma. I'm sure there's more to his sojourn than face value, but who knows. He could have just called. Whatever, I don't care, I love my Uncle R and it'll be great to see him. And now that I'm seven months pregnant, with a big bumping protruding tummy, I can't wait to see the look on my uncle's face.

Raj almost seems more excited than me about Uncle R's arrival. His sister, Parminder, is bringing him here.

Visitors.

Logan's Lament

"Education is when you read the fine print. Experience is what you get when you don't."
~Pete Seeger (1919 – 2014)

Although sometimes the time on the clock gets away on me, and I did not know what the *exact* time of night it was, I knew I'd better dig out my phone and call home. Best let Wendy know where I was because I promised her, and our new counsellor, that I'd try to be a better communicator. Of course, the call goes to her voicemail. "Please leave a message at the tone."

"Hi Wen, I'm just outside the hospital. I'm waiting for the night nurse to leave Shane's room. Soon as the light goes out, I'm going in. Ned's figured out the staff's schedule, and we are all cooperating with the hospital's staff, staying out of the way, and no more trouble. I've got big news. Ned says it's *confidential*, but I don't care. Who is Shane gonna tell? And you can do whatever you want, just don't tell your mother or Ned's mum. They both blabber all over town."

While I was waiting for the light to go out some weirdos walk by and give me their weirdo look. I know better than to engage. Maybe I look conspicuous lurking outside the hospital, spewing stupid words too loudly into my phone, but I don't care, it's *big* news.

"So, yeah, anyway, I know everyone says I'm not supposed to leave long rambling voicemail. Suffice to say I just found out my buddy brother from another mother, none other than one Rajinder Singh Gill is going to be a *father!* I'll tell you more when

I get home. I gotta go tell Shane now. The night nurse has turned the light out. Can you believe it, Raj, a dad? Okay, so, see you later-gator, love you."

Finally, the coast was clear, after what seemed like an eternity, the night nurse finished fiddling around in Shane's room and left. Soon as I got inside, I turned the soft lights on. Shane's eyes were open staring at the ceiling. Sometimes his eyes are open, sometimes they are closed. The doctors say we are not supposed to *infer* anything from this. "Open eyes do not necessarily convey any meaning of note."

Ned says these doctors don't know everything. "Everyone has a hypothesis. At this point they're all just guessing."

Last week I went to visit Shane late at night, turned the main light on, and there was Ned's mum sitting beside Shane, holding his hand. She says she prefers the lights off late at night because fluorescent lights are annoying and unhealthy. She left as soon as I got there. I *never* sit in the dark. I like the lights. Sitting in the dark seems weird. Besides that, I'll fall asleep without lights on.

"Yo, toe, toe, Shane," I touched the tip of his nose. Ned says tactile, auditory and visuals cues are helpful. So, I touch him, kiss him on the forehead and stuff. I never just sit there and hold his hand. He wouldn't like that. "You are *not* going to believe this. Uncle R went to India to parlay with Raj and Amelia. He wanted to talk to them in-person about you and your situation. But Ned says Uncle R likely had other reasons, and we will just roll with it. For some reason Uncle R didn't want to call them on the phone. It's an in-person preference. Anyhow, Raj's little sister, Parminder, is traveling with Uncle R. She's evidently a big help for him. Everyone's saying Uncle R has got some stuff he's dealing with, heh, don't we all, eh? Some deal better than others."

Suddenly one of Shane's monitor machines made a loud beeping sound. It's happened before, I know it's just measuring stuff, yet that stupid beep always scares me and makes me jumpy.

I always look over my shoulder with worry. I do it even when I know better. That's what Ned calls psycho conditioning, I guess.

"So, yeah, anyway, where was I? Oh right, so, Uncle R and Parmy Gill land at the Delhi airport. Where Raj and a seven-months pregnant Amelia are supposed to be meeting them. But they didn't, Raj sent a driver to catch them. Raj didn't want to leave Amelia home alone. And now that she's preggers, Amelia won't do any traveling on the India highways.

Anyhow when they got to Raj and Amelia's new house, they were both freaked out with extreme surprise and happiness. Because everyone has been worried about Uncle R and his aging weirdo issues, he had promised to call Ned straightaway after arriving to let Ned know everything's copacetic. Ned said when Uncle R called him, he was ecstatic. He's just ascreaming and snorting into the phone telling Ned that Amelia's *seven-months pregnant*."

I pulled up the hospital's sterile chair closer, sat down beside Shane, to deliver the kicker clause.

"And then Uncle R swears Ned on to the *Cone of Silence!* Really, he's not supposed to tell *anyone*. So, of course, Ned told me, and now I'm telling you. Shane, can you believe it, *Raj and Amelia are gonna have a kid. That means we are gonna be UNCLES!*"

Just then, like a metaphysic thing or a message from Zeus, my phone flashed again with *another* text message from Ned—"Remember, Cone of Silence."

"Oh man, Shane, do you remember the cone of silence stuff from when we were little kids? Ned *never* lifts the cone of silence. Unless, of course, he's telling you, or me, or Raj. Suppose Nina must be in his circle, but otherwise Ned's the best, eh. And you know I'm the worst offender."

Stupid machine beeps again, and again I jump. I don't know why it gets me every time.

"So, Shane, you gotta wake up buddy. There's a lot of stuff going on and we could use your help man." I did some sniffling and watery eye stuff.

"Forget the fuckin' Cone of Silence! If you told Ned's mum that she's gonna be a *grandma* no one's gonna get mad at you. You'd have a wide margin. It's different for me. My margin seems to be shrinking. Ned says it's Amelia and Raj's *prerogatives* as to who and when they tell people about the pregnancy."

I let out a big sigh.

"Hey, you know my Pops and I are doing really well these days. It's funny you know, most people hire babysitters to look after their kid. My Pops pays *me* money so he can look after Banny. It's good they love each other. Even my mum is doing better. I mean she's still extremely weird, but Banny brings us together. It's a good thing for everyone on all branches of the family tree. Besides, everyone loves Banny. The new counsellor seems to be helping Wendy and me. I'm trying to do better, but it's hard. I've been an asshole so long, changing is not easy."

I was getting ready to go when I remembered to tell Shane, "Oh yeah, and you gotta wake up because Ned says his mum has not only got you released from jail, but they have to give you bags of money for damages because they put you in a coma."

My phone buzzed again with another text message. It wasn't Ned this time, it was Wendy: When are you coming home?

"Shit Shane, I gotta get going home, Wendy's waiting for me."

Straightaway I sent her reply text: "Right Now—coming now."

I gave Shane a kiss on the forehead, "See you tomorrow buddy. I love you man. Please wake up, okay."

Got up to leave, picked up my jacket, put it on, and said, "I'm gonna turn the lights off now. Dark is good at night, right?"

Ned and Harpreet Dhaliwal

Seattle's Dave Niehaus (1935 – 2010) said,
"Progress always involves risk: You can't steal second base and keep your foot on first."

Historically, Nina and I have always had different biorhythms. Our circadian clock settings are often out of sync. She's an early bird, and I am not. If need be, I can get up early, but I would rather not. Logan and I were out late last night at Jenny's Cove Pub on Point Grey Road. They had the baseball game on the big screen. The game went into extra innings. History should have told me that it likely wasn't a good idea to let Logan buy a round of shooters. Nothing good comes after drinking a couple rounds of shooters. I should've stuck with beer. Peer pressure, and shooters are a bad combo. "Ned, how about another nightcap?"

At any rate, I did make it home well before breakfast. It was around three in the morning and Nina was sound asleep when I finally got home. I tiptoed in quietly. My head hit the pillow and I slept like a log. It was some time after nine in the morning, and I was in a deep, deep sleep, dreaming about when I was a kid playing T-ball. It was the best type of baseball for me. I loved smacking the ball off the Tee. In my dream I was getting ready to take a big swing when Nina started to try and wake me, "Ned, wake up." She gently rubbed my shoulder, lightly at first, and then with a little more force. "*Ned*, wake up!"

Stepping back from the batter's box, I began to regain a different level of consciousness, "What, Nina, what's happening?" I asked trying not to slobber.

"Mrs. Dhaliwal is downstairs; she wants to talk to you."

I woke up quickly, wondering, "Why is Harry's mother here?" At first, I figured Shane and Harry had got into some sort of mischief, *again*. Wouldn't be the first time those two have messed up, but then I remembered that Shane's in a coma. He's not going anywhere. Besides that, these days, I'm not their fixer anymore. After Shane took Harpreet to a séance to speak to Banny I quit trying to run interference. "Not in my job description."

Nina knew something was amiss with Mrs. Dhaliwal and was trying to be patient with my drowsy information processing. I smiled at Nina and said, "Okay, ok, you go talk to her, I'll get some clothes on." I kicked off bedding and got up on my feet with a slight wobble. I hate hangovers.

Nina nodded her head, smiled, and said, "Don't dawdle, get yourself put together, and come downstairs pronto. Capiche?"

"Yes, no, got it, I'll be down lickety-splitly." I pleaded with her.

I think Nina's still a little angry with me because last week we had a nine in the morning medical meeting. Nina woke me with adequate time to get ready. She went downstairs to wait for me to get together. I really did *start* to get myself together but put my head back on the pillow *for just a moment*. Next thing I know Nina is back in the room with a booming voice saying, "Ned, you are a *doofus*! Wake up."

Unfortunately, I had accidentally fallen back to sleep. "Oh, sorry Nina, what time is it?" I asked.

"Forget it, I'm going without you." She pivoted and stomped down the stairs. "Go back to sleep!" I glanced at the clock in the corner; it showed the time was only 8:32. That means I have got *plenty* of time before nine.

I quickly got myself dressed, and ready to go. However, when I got downstairs, Nina was long gone. She took the Mini Cooper, so I jumped on my road bike, and pedaled like crazy to the hospital. Deep down I knew that seldom do all the relevant doctors show up at the same time. They are always late. These things *never* start on time. Of course, this time it started on time. I tried to slide into the conference room quietly while Dr. Harrell was at the front of the room with a power point explanation of the *current* prognosis.

Today the room was quite full, everyone was there around the conference table. Fortunately, there was an empty seat beside Logan. No one wants to sit beside Logan. I slinked in beside him. "What did I miss?" I whispered to Logan.

He rolled his eyes, "Nothing has changed, nothing is happening, and these guys know *nothing*," Logan said loud enough for everyone to hear. He doesn't care. After all, he's Logan Meyers, he's rich and he doesn't care. Logan spends most of his time choralling and developing music theory.

Dr. Harrell shrugged, "Sorry Mr. Meyers, I understand your frustration. However, this is where we are at now. If there were something we could do, we would do it. Rest assured we are monitoring Mr. Bighill's condition and time will tell how this will result. It's not as though there is anything we can do to bring Shane out from the coma."

Nina sighed, "Thank you Dr. Harrell, we appreciate everything the team is doing." And with that the meeting adjourned. We did some hand shaking, glad-handing, see-you-laters, but Logan was right, nothing too bright on the horizon. Nothing has changed, and the likelihood of anything changing just doesn't seem to be something the *experts* can predict.

Sometimes, not always, I *overthink* stuff. Shane always said it's one of my shortcomings. "Trust your instincts," he'd say. "Don't overthink it."

When I was in first Year University, I suffered from a slight imposter syndrome. Not that I felt inferior or anything, I would sit in those freshman classes with a couple hundred other students, but I'd get lost and wonder "What's going on?" Everyone else seemed to know what was going on in the lecture. They're writing down notes, asking questions, and paying attention. I was watching girls and thinking about other stuff than the prof's pontificating power points.

Back then Shane was usually in between endeavours, and often on some type of court ordered probation, recognizance conditions, or legal supervision of some sort. So, Shane had time on his hands, and he started coming to classes with me. It was good. We'd go for a coffee, or a beer, afterwards, and talk about what the lecture's main points were all about. Shane really was a big help sliding me into the sophomore year. He helped me study. The best study buddy ever. I would overthink those stupid multiple-choice exams. Which was the *best response?* Was it A, B, C, D, or none of the above E, all of the above? I could never decide.

Shane said, "When in doubt pick C. Trust your initial inclination, do not overthink it." He got that from listening to Harpreet. Multiple choice exams suck. I wondered, "Is the right response the same as the best answer. Or was it simply sophomore semantics?"

I remember listening to Harpreet's augmented voice machine explain the way UBC works, and how he met Banny, "When I was a nineteen-year-old student at the University of British Columbia, I met Banerjee Malik. She was eighteen and the most beautiful woman I had ever seen in my life. Her hair was raven's black, shiny and long. Her eyes almond coloured, and a smile to light the room. Banny would tilt her head and nod with understanding at the important lecture points. We were in the same math class together. She sat two rows in front of me and one seat to the left. I could see she took lots of notes, listened closely, and seemed to understand everything Professor Wagner said and everything she wrote on the white board screen. I understood hardly anything and whatever notes I did take made no sense, but oh, oh, oh, that Banerjee Malik was the most beautiful woman I had ever seen. I tried so hard not to stare. It's bad manners to stare."

Over the years, Shane and Harry spent a lot of time together. I would get together with them as often as I could, but I always seemed to have too much stuff to do, with a deadline, too. So, if it wasn't one thing, it was another. And even though both of them told me not to stress about it, I kinda did so anyway. It's just the days turned to weeks, and weeks turned to months, and the next thing I know the time had slid by with me trying to keep my head above the waterline. "Don't get stressed about that stuff," Shane suggested. Harpreet honked his wheelchair's horn in support of Shane.

Harpreet was in the courtroom the day Shane was sentenced. He started honking his horn and wouldn't stop. Raj had to disconnect it while the sheriffs looked on with unhappiness. No order in the court, but at that point it was adjourned with Shane taken away in handcuffs.

So, there I was, I had three clean shirts laid out on the bed to choose from. I can always imagine Shane, sitting on my shoulder as a homunculus, he was shouting at me, "You are *overthinking* this."

But, on the other hand, I thought about it, and was positive because Mrs. Dhaliwal has *never* been here before. She's been to my mum's place a bunch of times, yet I don't remember her coming here before. Hence, an appropriate shirt is definitely in order, maybe buttons. I wouldn't want to look like a slob, right.

Only I don't want to be overdressing, either. Then that would make me look weird in my own place. Seriously, I'm just not a morning man. It's biorhythms and individual differences, that's what it's all about. We should celebrate not berate those who don't shine in the morning. Individual differences are *good.* If we were all the same, we'd all show up at the same restaurant, at the same time, and order the same dish. That'd be a problem. Again, individual differences are a good thing. I can get out of bed early, if I have the need or motivation. I was remembering how biorhythmic differences do...

From the bottom of the stairs Nina hollered, "Ned, pitter patter let's get at 'er! Mrs. Dhaliwal is waiting."

Grabbing my favourite red Albert Einstein T-shirt, I scrambled down the stairs without hesitation. However, as a long-standing perennial anthropological student of nonverbal communication I could see straight off something was looking less than desirable. "Hi Mrs. Dhaliwal," I gave her a hug. "How you doing?"

She started crying, "Harpreet died last night."

Now I wasn't expecting that, I was completely blindsided. "What are you saying?" I sort of shrieked. "I didn't even know Harpreet was sick! I just saw him last week, or maybe it was the week before, and he was fine. What the hell happened? How'd he die?"

In her life, Nina has suffered a lot of heartache, it's not that she is good at this stuff, but she is definitely better than me, by a lot. I know that sometimes, under stress, I might get a little reactionary.

We sat down and Mrs. Dhaliwal began to explain. Harpreet died from pneumonia. Although this seemed crazy to me, Nina confirmed that, medically speaking, this was not that unusual. Harry's immunodeficiency was a result of a variety of factors. Lifespan differs for everyone.

"He was only *thirty-seven!"* I moaned.

Thinking about it now, seems so long ago that Harry was nineteen years old when the Boy Scouts Camp Byng accident took place. That was over eighteen years ago now. Mrs. D thanked me profusely, saying because back then we had saved his life. We had given her more time with her son. She will always be grateful for that. We saved him, and kept him from dying that day, and for that she will forever be in our debt. Even though at this point I could not speak coherently, Mrs. D could feel my pain. Nina helped me out and chimed in by explaining how Harpreet enriched all of us, "We are so privileged to have known him. He made all our lives better."

We sat around for a while small talking when Mrs. D asked that we accompany her to the hospital to go talk with Shane. Using his computer augmented voice device, Harry always said Shane was his best friend, and it wasn't just because Shane saved his life all those years ago. It was the fact that Shane gave Harry a reason to live. After the accident, and as soon as Harry's health had improved enough to do stuff, Shane started taking him on *adventures.* They became best of friends. They got into various hijinks and mischief. I remember when they went to a séance. I thought it was less than worthwhile. Some thought it was stupid. Shane and Harpreet didn't care. They talked to dead people.

Don't know what I'd do without Nina, she leaned forward saying, "Yes, that's a good idea. I'll call Logan and tell him to meet us at the hospital. Unless, of course, if you'd like to call Logan, yourself?"

I knew I was still in no condition to talk to Logan with my voice breaking. I can't tell him that Harry is *dead.* "No, Nina, it's better you call him. I can't get through it. Logan would know something's up from my tone of voice. Raj always said it's the inflections, or the *hitch* in my voice that gives it away. I think it's best if you call him, thanks." And with that I started crying with convulsions, and more violently than I wished. It had hit me hard. "I'm sorry for all these tears Mrs. Dhaliwal, I loved Harry!"

She started crying, too.

Nina had walked out into the hallway and returned to deal with our tears. She'd been speaking with Logan. "He's going to meet us at the hospital in an hour."

"I should call Raj?" I wondered out loud.

Nina looked at the clock, "It's after eleven at night." She shook her head, "might be too late to call India?'

"Okay, if he doesn't pick up after two rings, I'll hang up." I *had* to call Raj. This isn't the Cone of Silence stuff. He was with us at Camp Byng when we first found Harry. He's got to know about Harry.

Nina slowly exhaled a confusing sigh, "The tones and ring-a-lings in India are different from here, you do what you think is best. Call Raj if you think you should."

Mrs. H.K. Dhaliwal

Plato said, "Wise men speak because they have something to say; fools because they have to say something."

Ned was trying to call us in India again, and I knew what he was on about. Yet I wasn't sure whether I should wake Amelia, she was napping. She's seven months pregnant and these days Amelia naps all the time. She'll nap in the morning, naps after lunch, naps before dinner, and then its real bedtime sleeping for eight hours or more. I'm sure it must mean something, but I don't know.

I re-opened the bedroom door as stealthily as possible, peeked in, and decided to wait for a while. I decided that Amelia was sleeping. Ned can wait; I'm not waking her. Then Amelia stirred, "Raj, what is it?" She moaned, "this is the *third* time in thirty minutes you've checked on me. Kee gal see?"

"Ned's calling, again, I'm sure it's about Harpreet."

"Yeah, what did he say?"

"I didn't answer."

"Why not?"

"He's your brother."

"He's your best friend."

"Nah, he was once, but nowadays Amelia, you're my best friend."

The thing was we already knew about Harpreet's passing for at least twenty-eight hours or so. It was just a matter of waiting for the others in our group to catch-up. Previously, we've had few false alarms. "Turns out there's more than one Harpreet Dhaliwal in the British Columbia's medical system data base!" Amelia exclaimed. "And one of them just died in Pouce Coupè."

"Where's that?" I asked.

"Northern British Columbia, just outside Dawson Creek."

"Guess I should have known better."

"Guess so."

Nevertheless, this wasn't really a completely illegal action or negative type of computer hacking, technically speaking, because Amelia still holds government authorized researcher status with the British Columbia provincial medical system research network, and she holds various data bank set access privileges. We programmed our home computer system to receive a notification alert from their network to ours. Whenever anyone named Harpreet Dhaliwal has medical information entered into the data bank's record system, we are notified. Of course, after a couple of false alarms we refined the coded program to alert us by entering *our* Harpreet's specific medical numbers. That took a bit of work. The generic approach failed and consequently necessitated an algorithm change.

"Amelia, how did you get those private medical coordinates?" I asked. Forgetting one of the basic principles involved with Amelia and her cyber skills: *if you are not ready for the answer, don't ask Amelia the question.*

So, one way or another, when we found out *officially,* the notification alert caught us completely off guard. He was *only* thirty-seven years old. Now, I realize, of course, same thing will happen for the others in our circle, too. Certainly, this information was not our prerogative to discuss with anyone, that right rested with Harpreet's family.

Consequently, when Amelia told me to call Ned, it was his narrative lead for me to follow, and *act surprised.* It indeed was duplicitous on my part, but what else was I going to do? Ethics are complicated.

Amelia snarled, "Raj, just *call* him. It's not even noon yet." Amelia said while rolling off the bed to get vertical albeit slowly.

Ned picked up the phone on the first ring, "Hey man, how you doing?" I planned on starting the conversation with a little *white* lie, "I saw that missed your call. I was doing nighttime cleanup rituals and had the phone's ringer off."

Ned sighed, exhaled, and groaned, "No problem, Raj. We got some stuff going on over here. Can you video call me in forty-three minutes?"

"Sure, forty-three minutes, you got it. What's up?"

"Mrs. Dhaliwal wants to hold a group meeting in Shane's hospital room. She wants to talk to all of us at the same time. Nina has arranged for us to meet with Logan, and she told him to bring his dad. We'll all be there in forty minutes. You and Amelia can attend via video feed."

"Okay."

"Okay, I'll connect you in when we get things setup." Ned let out a heavy sigh, "Needless to say, this is big, I need you in on time, forty minutes. Okay."

"Yes, yes, for sure, you got it, no problem. Forty minutes, I'll dial in."

Historically, Logan always reacts poorly to bad news. He's unpredictable, at the best of times. During a crisis don't count on Logan. When he was younger, Logan and his father had a terrible toxic relationship. That is, until Logan's baby daughter, Banny, was born. After Banny's birth they have bonded. They became quite close. Logan became a father, his pop a grandfather, and that was all it took for their never-ending angst to end. Maybe that analysis seems too simplistic, yet empirically speaking, it makes mathematical sense. Whatever, Nina was wise to suggest Logan should bring his father to the meeting. Leaving Wendy and toddler Banny back at home was a good idea. Likely Logan's going to react poorly to the news about Harry. I did.

~

Forty minutes, fast and slow, that's the way it goes. Don't worry Ned, I'll be on time. You can count on me.

~

When I was a university student I worked as a shelf stocker at my Uncle Mandeep's downtown drug and grocery store. Those days on the job the clock moved so slow. Boring jobs, I've had a few. Except the time when the shop got robbed. Excitement and endorphins flowed all over the place back then.

It was around ten at night, I was stocking shelves when this guy comes bursting in wearing a balaclava over his head. He starts screaming at the part-time high school cashier, Mary Peatman, to give him the cash. For some reason, which was well beyond my understanding, Mary was *hesitating*. I had to yell at her, "Mary, for fuck's sake, give him the money!"

They both looked at me. "Just give him the money Mary." I assured her, "It's okay, do it."

Really, you don't want to get stabbed over petty cash in the till. Besides, there's not much cash in the drawer anyway. Most people pay with plastic debit or credit cards. Besides, Uncle Mandeep is heavily insured. It's the cost of doing business. "Mary, give him the money!"

Mary opened the cash register drawer and backed away. The burglar leaped over the counter, grabbed the cash, and took off out the front door.

Just then, Amelia pokes my arm and jerks me out of my daydream, "Raj, forty minutes are up. Dial us in, eh?"

"Yes," I pulled myself together. "I'm on it."

Ned had strategically placed the video cam in the corner of the room so we could see everyone. It was a good angle, and the pixels were clear. Ned had a screen beside Shane's bed so everyone could see us. Shane looked so different to me. He had lost weight due to the vegetative state. Shane was once so big and strong. In my mind he was a giant. He didn't look so good today.

There were some introductory small talk pleasantries. Of course, everyone was duly shocked to see Amelia's seven-month low riding profile pregnancy bump. She was happy to show them. We reported that, "No we do not know the baby's gender and have shortlist of names to for each."

Then Ned gave the floor to Mrs. Dhaliwal to speak. It was weird for us at our end because we already knew she was going disclose about Harpreet. And even though I already knew it I could not contain my tears. I think I'd been holding back, and this was the time to let go.

As I expected, Logan took the news hard. Although Harpreet's death was sudden, evidently these things are not completely unexpected. One of Shane's doctors was there, and she explained how life expectancies work for Harpreet's complicated medical condition.

We lost the connection feed twice. And it was on their end, not ours. Our system is failsafe with backup. Anyway, we started disengaging and began to say goodbyes. Mrs. Dhaliwal was great.

She spoke directly to Shane. He was Harpreet's best friend *ever*. Even in his current vegetative state I just felt as though Shane could hear us. Whatever doesn't matter because Mrs. Dhaliwal was clearly happy to see Amelia's baby bump. A new life coming.

They were planning a formal ceremony for Harpreet, but everyone understood that given Amelia's bump and our India timeline we would not attend.

It was a sad situation. None of us will ever forget Harry. He taught us a lot. Can't believe he's gone.

And there's Shane, wonder how long this can go on? Hope he comes out of this coma soon.

Part Four

MISSIVES, MESSAGES & POSTS

"To see ourselves as others see us is a most salutary gift. Hardly less important is the capacity to see others as they see themselves."
~Aldous Huxley (1894 – 1963), *The Doors of Perception.*

Autocorrect meets Kelsey

Dearest Parm,

I'm going old school here, writing you an old-fashioned pen and paper long handed letter. I know an email is more likely to arrive to you in India, but this is therapeutic for me. Whatever, mostly I'm trying to sort it all out in my own head by writing to you. Call it writing therapy or therapeutic writing. It's not journaling!

I got your brother's mailing address from Ned Reilly. I simply called him saying, "Hi, its Kelsey Pearce. Do you have a surface mailing address for Parm's brother Raj?" Ned was happy to help. I figured Raj would get this missive to you. Ned was skeptical about surface mail, yet he was encouraging, nonetheless.

Ned is completely stressed out about Shane Bighill's coma. That whole thing is another strange story with no end in sight. A sad situation for sure. Hope some sort of a happy ending happens soon, this all seems doubtful to me. But what do I know anyway? Tough stuff to try and figure out, eh?

So, today's story starts with the first episode beginning last week when Caitlyn Chan calls me and asks to meet up for lunch. She says she wants to introduce me to her new *partner*, named: Autocorrect.

"Her name is Autocorrect," I asked.

Caitlyn says no and yes. Autocorrect is her nickname. Her birth certificate name is Carol Wilson, but everyone *calls* her Autocorrect.

I asked, "What happened to Joel?"

Caitlyn explained that they broke up because when she came out as bisexual, Joel couldn't cope with the news. I understand he got a little angry feeling like some duplicity had happened. He takes stuff personally.

Did you know Caitlyn is bisexual? *I didn't know.* She said you knew, and she thought you must have told me so, but you didn't. Wish you were here. Wish we could talk. Wish you could have come to the luncheon with Autocorrect, CC, and me. It would have been better if you had been there to help me understand what it all means. You've always been better at interpreting, decoding, and understanding weirdness. Compared to me, you ace that stuff. I get lost in the quagmire too easily.

Please don't get me wrong; I'm of course quite copacetic with Caitlyn coming out as gay, bisexual or whatever. Love is *always* a good thing. Yet why do you think everyone calls her new partner, Autocorrect? I found out at the luncheon. She's domineering, loud, and bossy. All the traits I find awfully annoying, but Caitlyn says she *love*s Autocorrect. Now they are living together. So, as long as they are together, for sure, Autocorrect gets a *pass* from me. Who am I to judge anything? If Caitlyn likes being bossed around and dominated, that's her business.

Business—remember when Edilma and I had that BIG spat about science versus business? I swear she started it. Someone said, "Don't take it personally, it's just business." That shit pissed me off!

Now I know sometimes I can go a little wingy over something without warrant. But Edilma defended the concept saying we should acknowledge and honour entrepreneurs more. "Business makes the world turn." Big red flag for me because my side says science is more important. No one says, "Don't take it personally, it's *just science*." Like it's okay to screw people over when it's business. Scientists have ethics. Entrepreneurs want to make money. That's all they are about, that's business. I'm not as confident about free markets and capitalism. Edi endorses it. She thinks it is a good thing.

Anyhow, you know how long it took us to recover—too long! Edilma is a Latina. Everybody knows Latinas are bad for tempers and grudges, eh. Mind you, I wasn't much better. Edilma and I are copacetic now, and we've made up. In fact, other than to tell you about the lunch date with Autocorrect, I'm writing to let you know that Edi has invited me to go to *Puerto Rico*. She's with this artsy group project that has landed a Canadian federal grant seed money endowment to develop an arts and infrastructure programme in Puerto Rico. Although my Spanish isn't perfect, Edi says it's passable for this project.

I met with the organizers yesterday, and the project looks good. So, I'm in, and leaving for Puerto Rico in three weeks. I signed up for a two-month stint, with an option to renew. I've got the time, and the skills. So, we'll see how it goes.

Consequently, when you get back to Vancouver, I'm going to be long gone. Maybe you can come visit. Hope so.

Let's stay in touch.

Love and hugs,

Kelsey

P.S—give CC a call, or send her an email, something—I know she'd love to hear from you! She says she's worried about you, yet cryptically enough; she's the one living with Autocorrect (lol).

NO SNAIL MAIL

From: Parminder K. Gill (parm@Gill-AI.com)

To:Kelsey Pearce (kelseypearce@hotsmail.com)

RE:Gup Shup

Hey Kelsey, after all these years, you are still way too cool for school. Yesterday my brother brought me the snail mail letter handwritten that you sent all the way from Vancouver. Thanks so much! It's a Special Delivery—because it's from YOU.

I'm sending this return epistle electronically. Of course, I don't have your surface land address for hard copy snail mail in Puerto Rico. Who knows how their snail mail works anyway? Hence, email always works well because you've never changed your e-address since we were kids. My new e-addy is connected to Raj's research institute. He's calling me an "associate." He's not money laundering per sé, but I'm getting paid rupees to do pedestrian research gopher tasks and simple data analyses for him. Anyone could do it, but the nod goes to me. I'm employed.

I've been in India for the past two weeks and staying for at least another two. I'd stay longer, but I've got to get back to UBC. My academic advisor is sending emails asking about my assignment's progress (they have stalled, but that's not what I'm telling Professor Julson).

Good News—I now know the complete history of email. My brother paid me big bucks to accompany Amelia's Uncle R to India. I didn't really want to do it, but Raj said he'd do anything for Uncle R, anything. After that, what could I say? They wanted to make sure he arrived in India without incident. He speaks some Punjabi but doesn't know his way around things very well. He is a little awkward and gets confused easily. He tends to turn right when he should go left—metaphorically and physically so to speak. Left-handed issues.

I love, love, love, my sister-in-law! Amelia is so smart, talented, and just lovely. She gives the gears to Raj when he needs poking, and that's always to my delight. All my life Raj has been the smartest person I've ever known (next to Kelsey Pearce—who got me through Organic Chem 210, and I'm forever grateful). Now I have a sister. She extends our family by a kilometre.

The last time I saw you was at the Vancouver airport—thanks for the ride. Since then, it's been quite an adventure. While we were travelling, Uncle R explained the detailed complete history and development of email: ad nauseam, ad infinitum, and to the mathematical nth degree. Evidently, he was an early adopter from mainframe CPU to current cell phones. At first, I found him awfully annoying. He pontificates all the time. He's a professional talker. Nevertheless, after a while, he began to grow on me. He does know a lot of interesting trivia, and some science. Now we are BFFs. I've never had a senior citizen BFF before. It's fun.

Raj insists, technically speaking, Uncle R's chronologically only sixty-three, and in Canada, the federal government decrees at sixty-five years old a person is officially old. Whatever, Uncle R is an old white guy with foibles and eccentricities. Having said that, however, in India, there are a lot of perks travelling with an old white basorg. When he shows up the crowds' part for him and let him pass through easily, with me holding on to his coattails. If I'm by myself, different story, I've got to fight, squeeze, and elbow my way along to get through the dense Indian throngs. He likes riding the bus and trains. I can't take the bus by myself, but with him things are easier.

"Namaste, I'm Dr. Reilly, this is my assistant, Parminder Gill." Easy peazy we move to the front of the line—back of the caboose sucks.

Tall old white-hair guys get preferential treatment in India. Uncle R sticks out in a crowd. When we are together, we get to enter in the first-class lineups. There are often special lines for tourists. It's good. Indians are deferential because they want him to be happy and feel good about being here. It's just the way it is and always will be—India.

Your lunch with Caitlyn and her new partner, Autocorrect, sounded interesting. Wish I could've been there with you, for moral support, if nothing else. Although I had some sexuality suspicions with Caitlyn, I really know nothing about these things. There was a time I thought Caitlyn was hitting on me, but my social skills are weak at best. What do I know about sex? I come from a sheltered background. I'm not worldly like you. At any rate, I wish the best for them. Love conquers all.

So, okay, that's about all the gup shup (English translation—gossip and social commentary) I've got from Northern India. Stay in touch.

Hope you enjoy Puerto Rico—what an adventure!

Pack lots of sunscreen.

Send me some email pics.

Love and hugs,

Parm

PS—I will give Caitlyn a call.

Arrived Safe and Sound

From: Dr. Randal Reilly (Randal@ReillyPsych.com)

To: Harjit K. Sidhu (HSidhu@BCcourts.com)

Annette Reilly (Annette@Reilly-Law.com)

RE: Arrived Safely

Hello from Chandigarh!

First thing to say is how terribly sad it was to hear about Harpreet's passing. Soon as we arrived at Chandigarh, Raj explained Harpreet's death through some tears and sniffles. Raj said the boys back home were devastated to hear the news. Evidently, Ned and Mrs. Dhaliwal arranged for a video teleconference in Shane's hospital room to let everyone know about Harpreet's passing.

Sorry it has taken a few days to touch base with you two. Hence a joint email to update you both simultaneously. Raj gave me a new phone and laptop.

What with all the travel time involved, Indian travel connections, and extreme jet lag, it's been quite an adventure, to say the least. I'm not sure what day it is today anyway. Doesn't matter, they're all the same. It's Blursday. Nevertheless, I finally arrived safe and sound in the Punjab. Amelia and Raj live in a big house in a lovely city called Chandigarh. It was a long trip; however, I am happy to be here in Chandigarh. It is warm, and awfully hospitable. Good food, too.

Turns out it was indeed a good idea to upgrade the flight to travel business class because the twelve thousand kilometres distance, and sixteen hours flying time does indeed take a toll.

It is an awfully long period of time to sit in a metal tube, flying a gazillion miles per hour over the North Pole to arrive on the other side of the world. I haven't developed a fear of flying or anything. It's just that everything seems harder these days. Maybe it is my age getting the better of me. I am not getting any younger.

Fortunately, for me, Raj Gill's younger sister, Parminder, was on the same flight to New Delhi. Parm has been a big help getting us out of the busy airport in Delhi. Then we had to drive to Amelia and Raj's house in Chandigarh. Originally, the plan was that Raj would meet us at the Delhi airport and he was supposed to bring us to Chandigarh. However, as soon as we landed Parminder's cell phone started pinging and ringing. Raj was sending her messages saying he was not able to meet us. Rather, he had retained a driver who would take us the four-hour drive to Chandigarh. Turns out Raj said he had some medical issues to deal with and could not leave town.

We got through customs and immigration without too much hassle retrieved our luggage—Parm could not believe how heavy my bag was—and we made our way outside into the New Delhi air. Parminder is a strong kid.

Let me tell you the cacophony of the inside of the Delhi airport was nothing compared to the outside. A lot of people were milling about. Parm could tell it was all getting a little overwhelming for me. She pointed out that I keep turning the *wrong* direction. Definitely a neurological deficiency, or a left-handed tendency. Parm found a safe spot for me to stay put until she could locate the driver.

Within a couple minutes Parm gave me the two fingers in the mouth whistle and waved me to come towards her. The driver was holding a sign that read in large black letters: Uncle R and Parm Gill. The car was deep in the Delhi airport parking lot. After some maneuvering, we found it. They loaded the luggage in the back, seemed as though they were arguing in Punjabi, but Parm said no, that's just how they discuss the situation. Loudly. No reason to be concerned.

Next thing I knew we were starting the four-hour drive (with various shortcuts thrown in to avoid tolls) to Chandigarh. Just getting out of Delhi was something else. The air smells and tastes pungent, all the cars keep honking horns - for no reason discernible to me. Regardless, we were finally on our way. Using millennial speak, Parm said that it was *all good.* Also, "just trust the driver" was her frequent mantra. Although I had heard that mantra before, coming from her it was helpful, somewhat.

Thanks to Buddha, Zeus, Krishna, and all the other gods, because it was fortunate that Parm was there to help me. Otherwise, I would have had been in some travel trouble. Things are harder than I thought they'd be. Life's like that, unfortunately. John Lennon said the same thing in one of the Beatle's songs, "It's getting harder all the time."

Back to the road trip - eventually, after too many twists, turns, bumps and constant incessant horn honking, we arrived in Chandigarh—Sector 5A.

Our driver beep beeped his horn and the gate to their residence opened. Raj and Amelia emerged from the house; it became clear why Raj did not meet us at the Delhi airport. Amelia is *pregnant*! I thought about to give birth any moment now, but they informed me she is only *seven* months pregnant. This is not my area of expertise, but Amelia has blossomed!

Now you two know me better than anybody on this planet, but recently, somewhere along the way, I have become a bit of a crybaby. Have you noticed? I wasn't like this before, but when I saw Amelia standing on their front stoop, the tears came and I just started crying, like a big baby. Wasn't really anything but happy tears. Still, I was caught off guard, I wasn't expecting to see my niece in full bloom.

I'm going to be a *great uncle.* Amelia says I have always been a great uncle to her—even though she says she knows Ned is my favourite nephew. I replied, Ned is my *only* nephew.

Now, I'm not speaking out of turn, or breaching any level of confidentiality, Amelia says I can tell whomever I wish about her pregnancy. It's not a secret, no confidentiality clause here. Evidently, they disclosed to Ned, Nina, Logan, his father Gerry, and Mrs. Dhaliwal at the recent video teleconference in Shane's hospital room. Obviously, Mrs. Dhaliwal was happy to see Amelia's big pregnancy bumper. You know, the idea that with one life leaving the planet and another entering made her feel positive karma.

Okay, so I must sign off now, and put on my traveling clothes. Raj has arranged for another driver to take Parm and me to Ludhiana this morning for some sort of family function that he does not wish to attend. Originally it was planned that Raj would go with Parm, however, under the current circumstances with Amelia's condition, he is not going anywhere. They think I am a better substitute anyway. Everyone is kind to old white-haired, white guys here in India.

I am having a very good time, glad to be here, the weather is lovely, and will keep you posted.

All good wishes and smiles,

Love,

Randal

Motherhood and Secrets

From: Ned Reilly (Nedreilly@gmail.com**)**

To: Uncle Randal (Randal@ReillyPsych.com**)**

RE: Motherhood and Secrets

hey Uncle R, guess your cell phone has crashed, or you've "*misplaced*" it, again.

I'll call Raj, he'll help you install an Indian SIM card. Don't pay traveling British Columbia roaming fees, eh—waste of dough.

Whatever, I know you chronically check email frequently wherever you are. Thus, this is the deal—an email update.

Just want to say, thanks man, I appreciate you disclosing Amelia's pregnancy to my mum (your sister). I've been sitting on the situation for a couple days now feeling bad about the whole confidentiality thing. I don't like keeping big secrets from mum. It always makes me uncomfortable—she's my mum. She's a weirdo, but she's my mum. We have history. She needed to know her change of pending status to grandma.

Nina insists its Amelia's prerogative to tell people about the pregnancy, not *mine*. And you know how often Dr. Nina Bighill is correct, compared to me.

All my life I've been dealing with Amelia and mum's mother/ daughter psychoses. They're so competitive. One is always trying to be weirder than the other.

On the other hand, at least Nina is normal, and that's nice. We're doing fine, and I hope you enjoy your Indian sojöurn. Raj says you are accompanying Parm to their aunt's funeral death ceremony because he can't go. Most likely, he doesn't want to go, Amelia's pregnancy notwithstanding. After all these years, Raj and his Pop still bicker quite a bit.

Okay, it's applied anthropology, I'm going to be an *uncle.* That makes you a *great uncle.* And you are a great uncle.

Give my best to Raj and Amelia. Be nice to Parmy. She's a good kid.

Remember, don't be weird with civilians—they won't understand.

Love,

Ned

PS—call me with your new phone number.

I still can't believe Raj and Amelia are going to be *parents.*

I'll keep you posted if there are any updates with Shane—nothing has changed since you left.

Part Five

SHRINKS SAY WHAT

"The scientist is not a person who gives the right answers; the scientist is the one who asks the right questions."

~Claude Lévi-Strauss (1908 – 2009)

Professional Psych Executor

If you cannot find peace within yourself, you will never find it anywhere else.
~Marvin Gaye (1939 – 1984)

"Uncle R, you have way too much luggage," Amelia said, shaking her head, transferring some clothes from my big bag to her smaller travel bag. "You don't need to take *everything* on this trip with Parmy."

My niece, Amelia, was helping with wardrobe selection and re-packing. They had asked if I could accompany Raj's sister, Parminder, to a traditional Indian funeral service in Ludhiana. From there we were going to travel to the Golden Temple in Amritsar. Raj did not want to go anywhere leaving Amelia behind in late-stage pregnancy. Although Amelia makes like she is not anxious about childbirth, she makes it clear that she is not leaving the house until it's time to go to the hospital. So of course, I said it would be my pleasure to go to Ludhiana. I've never been there before and helping Parminder is a bonus because she has been a godsend to me.

"Listen Uncle R, it's okay to stick out a little, but not too much." Amelia held up one of my shirts, "You won't need a plaid flannel shirt, it's too hot for that. Why did you bring two ties?"

I shrugged, "I always pack two ties, a houndstooth one and blue silk tie. One never knows when wearing a tie is needed for a function. It's an old habit, I guess, and you know that old habits die hard."

Although I did not want to look like Justin Trudeau when he traveled to India, Prime Minister Trudeau went overboard with local clothing costumes. Learning from his example I didn't want to look weird. "Amelia, I'm not a fuddy duddy."

"Okay, but sometimes cargo shorts are inappropriate in India."

Nowadays, Raj and I are close enough to the same size in clothing. So, some of his Indian ceremonial clothes were put in my bag.

"Parm will help you with appropriate clothes. She knows whats what."

Just as Amelia was holding out my second favourite pair of jeans saying these were the kind of jeans Barack Obama was criticized for wearing - *mom jeans.* Raj came into the room waving and holding out a cell phone. "Uncle R, you need to call your wife," Raj said, waving the phone in front of me. "Ned called asking me to get you setup with an Indian SIM card and a new phone number. This is it."

"Did he say why?" I asked.

Raj smiled, "Why do you need to call home, or why do I need to fix you up with a new Indian phone number?"

"Both."

"Well, as I understand it, a number of people are calling your Vancouver cell number, leaving messages, and you aren't responding."

"Yes Raj, that's because I'm still on the airplane mode with roaming and ringer off, as instructed by my techie nephew, Ned."

"No problem," Raj smiled. "You can use this phone it's all set up and ready to roll. You can call, text, surf the net, or take pics, whatever you want. You are good to go."

Amelia was not going to be left out of the conversation, "So, you know that it's wrong to call Vancouver now, right?"

"Why's that?"

With a kindly smile, Amelia reminded me, "Well, it is almost noon here, and with Vancouver's daylight-saving time conversion, it's two in the morning there. Therefore, not a good time to call."

Nodding my head in agreement, "I'll email Harjit with the new SIM card phone number saying she can call me, anytime, day or night. How's that?"

"Perfect."

Parminder had come up the stairs. She knocked on the door frame, "Don't want to break up the party, but the driver is here. Also, Raj, mummy has left me two messages, and Pops has called three times. We should hit the road, eh?"

"What was her message?" Raj asked.

"What do you think?" Parm smiled. "She wants to know where we are, and when will we get there?"

"Did you tell her I'm *not* coming?" Raj asked.

Parm shook her head, "Nope, not my responsibility, you talk to them. After all, you are their number one son."

"Maybe later, much later," Raj tapped her shoulder, made gurgling groaning sound, then he went downstairs to talk to the driver.

~

To say driving in India is the opposite from driving in Canada is more than an understatement. And it's not just that the driver's steering wheel is on the opposite side of ours, or that they drive on the other side of the road. "Raj, why do they bother to have lines painted on the road if no one pays any attention to them," I asked?

Raj simply smiled, "Don't worry about it, it's just the way traffic works. We've got a lot of people to move about here in India.

Just think of it as a type of organized confusion. It works." He held his palm up in the air, "It's just traffic, don't worry about it.'

Amelia gave me a big hug, "Trust the driver," she whispered in my ear, and with that we were on our way down the road. Her reasoning, as she patiently previously explained to me, "The driver may *seem* reckless, yet, of course, he doesn't have any desire to crash the car. It's his job. He doesn't want to screw it up."

Amelia knows that unlike her mother, I don't have a fear of flying, but I have been developing some sensitivities with driving. I get nervous. The social contract where you stay on your side of the road and I on mine seems to be breached too often. Too many people are crazy drivers.

When I was a young up-and-coming under paid psychologist, with a mortgage, and too many bills to pay, I often took on several patients who held a fear of flying. It was good work, more often than not, I was able to help some of these patients overcome their fears and fly on a commercial airplane. We used cognitive mind restructuring behaviour therapies, as well as basic Skinnerian systematic desensitization techniques.

Back in those days the British Columbia Psych Association and the Western Canada Airlines had agreements where a vetted list of registered licensed psychologists could use their airplanes for therapy purposes. The airlines want folks to fly. It's business.

The shrinks who held official airline permission could take patients on board an empty parked airplane to do some therapy. Before actually boarding a plane we always had a few preliminary therapy sessions to prepare for the next level. In the first field sessions we had been sitting in the parking lot just off the Airport Boulevard to watch airplanes taking off, and landing. Usually, I would have two patients in the Volvo's backseat and one in the front passenger seat. Group therapy work was a good way to discuss their phobias and fears.

We would watch airplanes from the boulevard. There were always lots of big ones taking off and landing. "Oh, wow, look at that Boeing 838 taking off," I'd point up to the sky. "They're probably going to Hawaii or somewhere exotic. Wish I was with them, all this Vancouver rain is getting depressing."

More than once I've had a patient say, "Thanks, doc, depressing rain, eh? You got pills?"

"Yes, very few people think rain is therapeutically helpful to assist psychotherapy. Here comes the sun—now that's encouraging."

Next, we'd physically move into the airport, walk around, have coffees and talk about traveling. Then we would board an empty Western Canada Airlines jet, put on seatbelts, recite our mantras and think about flying. Just like clinical hypnosis, these techniques didn't work for everyone, but it did for some. And that's a good thing. "You can lead a horse to water, but you can't make her drink." This was like that.

~

Today, in India, as I was going to get in the chauffeur driven car, I thought to myself, "Our driver looks awfully old." However, as Amelia explained it, "Listen, seriously, an experienced driver, like Mr. Lakhbir Singh Narwal, is preferable to younger, risk taking hotshot drivers. Trust me on this. I know about these things."

Of course, I trusted Amelia's opinion, but I was still nervous about the traffic and congestion. Mathematical applied Bayesian probability theory bothered me. I tried to explain the math principles to Parm once we were settled in the backseat. I sat behind the driver, Mr. Narwal, while Parm sat in the "*power seat*" on the other side of me to converse, listen, and debate driving traffic strategies with Mr. Narwal. Although Parm's power seat explanation seemed weird to me because she's from Vancouver, who am

I to question anything. I was nervous about the traffic. Too many horns honking.

"Okay," I clarified to Parm. "As the crow flies, it's one hundred and twenty kilometres to Ludhiana, according to Raj it should take a little over two and a half hours to get there. And we're traveling mid-day. Yet, it's heavy traffic here all the time. Not like in Vancouver where there's a definite rush hour in the morning and evening. So, according to theory, sooner or later we're going to buy it and get in a crash."

"That makes absolutely no sense to me," Parm said, scrunching up her face. "Besides, I think that kind of negativity just invites problems irrespective of *probability theory.* You are looking for problems!"

I was beginning to explain the parameters of the principles underpinning the mathematics theory when the new cell phone Raj gave me started ringing, vibrating, and buzzing. Raj had programmed the device to make certain I would not miss any calls with all these notifications. However, as a failsafe, Raj also had voicemail to text transcript activated.

It was my wife, Harjit, calling. I was hoping it was good news about Shane. It wasn't. She was calling to deliver some *bad* news about my old friend, Arthur Sutherland. Seems he has intentionally taken his life. Evidently, a few days passed before anyone noticed that there was an odour coming from his apartment. Someone alerted the authorities.

Harjit said Arthur had left a suicide note mentioning my name, number, and address. She found this out when the police arrived at our house with three boxes of Arthur's old client psychology files. Guess I had forgotten to tell Harjit that I was listed as Arthur's professional executor with the British Columbia licensing board of psychologists. I explained that as part of the license application process each new applicant must supply the board with the name of a current licensed psychologist who will attend to the deceased's practice in the event of their death. I was trying to help Artie get back on his feet in British Columbia. Of course, I agreed to serve as his psychology professional executor. It was the least I could do for Artie. He was a dear friend of mine.

"Harjit, remember when Derek, your hairdresser, died?" I reminded her how devastating receiving the news of his death was to her. She had a previously scheduled hairstyle appointment with Derek for the following week. It got cancelled when she got the news from the manager of the hair salon. Rita was calling all of Derek's clients to deliver the news and offer an alternate hairdresser.

Same thing happens in psychology, everyone's professional executor must get a hold of current patients to notify and assist with alternate arrangements, if required. Past patients are a different story. That's what the three boxes were about. Those were his past patients. Due to his recent legal problems, I knew that Arthur did not have many, if any, current patients. It was a plan that never materialized. Thus, no pressure on me.

Arthur's sister was scheduled to come up from Santa Monica to deal with all the other death details. She must make arrangements for the body, formal legal procedures, and all his apartment's stuff. All I have to do is take possession of three boxes of psychology files. There won't be a funeral service because that was his desire. That's fortunate because I'm not big on funerals anyway.

Poor Arthur, I'm sorry he decided to check out of this life at age sixty-three. I remember the great comedian Robin Williams also intentionally took his life at age sixty-three. Both had health issues, but only they know their own personal dynamics that pushed them to do the final deed. I miss them both—gone too soon.

My shoulder was being tapped, or something was poking me.

"Hey, Uncle R," it was Parminder poking my shoulder. "Time to wake up, okay."

"I'm awake."

She gave me a quizzical look, "Are you okay?"

"Hon jee, atcha, yes, I'm fine."

"Oh good, you're speaking Punglish," she nodded. "Amelia instructed me to give you periodic mental status questions."

"Really."

"Yeah, she says everyone is worried about you, and now I'm supposed to be keeping an eye on you. Make sure you are copacetic with everything."

"How am I doing?"

She smiled, "So far, so good. Do you know where you are?"

"Middle of nowhere."

Our driver, Mr. Lakhbir Singh Narwal, snorted. Turns out he understands more English than I was led to believe.

Parminder ~ Shrinks Say What

"Where id is, there shall ego be."
~Sigmund Freud (1856 – 1939)

Although, historically, I often find that old white guys are usually awfully privileged and terribly annoying, Uncle R, however, was starting to grow on me, and it's not just because my brother Raj gets emotionally glassy eyed at the mention of his name. Uncle R and Raj have a long history, and a big bond from all those years ago when they were camping with the Boy Scouts. They shared a critical incident together when Banerjee Malik and Harpreet Dhaliwal had a suicide pact gone wrong. But that's a whole other long streamed story, for another time.

Suffice to say, my brother Raj is awfully fond of Uncle R.

Of course, Raj's wife, Amelia, thinks the world of her Uncle R, she's known him all her life. He's her favourite uncle. Separately, and together, they both took tag-turns talking to me about the upcoming road trip with him. My brother is a pro lecturer.

I tried to explain to them, "I've *already* been with Uncle R since the sixteen-hour airplane flight from Vancouver to New Delhi, the seemingly never-ending taxi road trip from Delhi to Chandigarh, and altogether that's a lot of time to spend with a talkative pontificating old guy. Yes, I understand, he's a bit quirky, but we'll be fine. It's not a *big* thing. Besides, he's starting to grow on me."

And, additionally, on the other hand, I actually do *need* him. I can't very well travel to Ludhiana solo, and not have my Pops go unnecessarily wingy dingy beserkoe. "Young girls do *not* travel alone in India." And if I replied with, "I'm a twenty-three-year-old *woman*, not a little girl," Pops would react predictively with a hostile rebuttal. So why bother bickering. Life is too short.

Raj baits me saying, "Sure, go ahead, and tell Pops why Uncle R is accompanying you and not me. No problem, I don't care."

Oh, sure, no worries, it'll be a problem all right, yet not my problem. Pops will get all huffy and puffy emphasizing, "Raj, should be here. It is his *duty*." Father-son stuff is beyond my level of comprehension. Raj and Pops have always had their own peculiar dance steps. I think it's them. It's not an Indian thing. Whatever, I try to not get involved. And when I do, mother serves as an intermediary. For one thing, I know that she'll be simply ecstatic with the news of becoming a grandmother. Who knows how Pops will react? I don't care. Doesn't matter, I didn't travel alone, so he can't get angry with me. He's always getting apoplectically angry at Raj.

Uncle R is sixty-three, and I'm twenty-three years old. That's a forty-year, four-decade difference in our ages. So, certainly, we look at life differently. Whatever, Uncle R came through for me when I needed him. I had committed to my parents, and extended family, that for sure I'd attend the Antam Sanskaar end of life ritual honouring Chaachee, my auntie who died from extreme old age.

While I am no thanatologist, this death ceremony was my first formal thing, and I really hoped it would go okay. Dozens of cousins, aunts, and uncles from all over the diaspora had gathered to celebrate Chaachee's completion of life ceremony.

Once we finally arrived in Ludhiana, we changed clothes at my cousin, Ishan's house, and then he took us the rest of way to the temple. Ishan drives fast, but he knows where we need to go, and how to get there. He's very trustworthy.

Fortunately, Amelia had helped with Uncle R's wardrobe selection. She said, originally, he had planned on wearing a traditional blue blazer, white shirt and tie ensemble. She re-arranged his luggage and packed some appropriate clothes. He still stands out, but he looks fine, nothing too weird or unseemly. He's an attractive old white guy. People are always looking at him. He's oblivious to the attention. Of course, I introduced him to my family, and everyone else, as Dr. Reilly from Vancouver. And explained that I was his research assistant and traveling companion in India. "He's writing a book."

Evidently, one of Raj and Amelia's biggest concerns was that Uncle R has recently been showing some signs of getting easily disoriented and confused. Although I have not personally seen any evidence of this stuff, I figured he was just a bit eccentric, and that was the situation. He was fine as far as I was concerned, just an example of the classic absent-minded professor syndrome.

When we were in Chandigarh, I noticed that Raj would often take hold of Uncle R's hand when crossing the street, going into a restaurant, or maneuvering through a crowd. So, I started doing the same thing. It was easy to keep track of him that way. As a pedestrian from Canada, our traffic instincts are reversed, and this can be problematic. And to make things worse, Uncle R is left-handed. He often turns the wrong direction and goes the wrong way. He claims it's a right hemisphere parietal lobe neurological thing. Amelia agrees with him, so what do I know anyway? Amelia has a medical degree.

Apparently, directionality is a genetic neurological thing. Amelia says you can blindfold some people, spin them around, take off the blindfold, and ask them to point north. People with strong cerebral directionality have no problem. Uncle R says, north, south, west, whatever, it's too abstract for him. Directions don't mean much to Uncle R. Guess he's a divergent thinker or something. He seems so smart.

Sometimes it appears like we were holding hands all the time. But it was no big thing. Not like with Wes Roberts, my sorta for-a-while, boyfriend, who thought handholding was the gateway to further romantic acts. I don't miss Wes anymore.

In real life back home, Uncle R works as a psychotherapist. Here in India, it's all quite surreal. Different culture, customs, language and whatnot, all makes everything seem surreal. I'm spending so much time with Uncle R when I finally realized it would be a good idea to take advantage of the situation. Free therapy.

"So, you don't think I am sexually confused?" I asked.

"Do you think you are sexually confused?"

He often answers a question with a question. I assumed that was part of his therapeutic technique. I talked to him about Wes and the whole heterosexual dance steps. Then I talked to him about Caitlyn Chan and my sexual encounter with her, and what it might mean, or not.

"I had sex with Wes, a few times, five to be precise, twice in one night. Didn't actually have sex with Caitlyn, but I'm sure it was a sexual experience," I explained. "Well, sex, what do I know anyway? I come from a sheltered background. How about you?"

"What about me?"

"What do you know about sex?" I asked.

"What would you like to know?"

"For starters, could you quit answering a question with a question."

"Okay." He nodded his head, but I had my doubts.

On our next leg of the road trip, we drove the busy highway to visit the Golden Temple in Amritsar. Along the way we talked about individual differences, sensory thresholds, and existentialism. It was good. He got me thinking about things that were from a different angle than what I had presumed. Uncle R is a wise guy (for an old fart). And I mean it in a good way.

He explained the sensory thresholds theory thing saying some people have different needs, desires, and motivations. It's certainly neurological, but sociological, too. Everyone needs to eat food, but some people eat to live whereas others live to eat. I didn't get it at first. Made sense after some thinking. Some people have the need for speed, others like to take it slow: it's a continuum, not binary.

Raising my index finger to make the point, I explained, "Okay, so, of course, no one is going to say they don't *like* sex, right. That would make you appear weird, nonconforming or socially undesirable. Yet, I don't know if sex is the be-all-end-all thing that Wes tried to sell me when he quickly climaxed asking: How was it for you?"

Uncle R tilted his head, and said, "Well, how was it for you?"

"Ugh, there you go again! You *always* answer a question with a question. Besides, I was being rhetorical with Wes' by saying the how was it for you thing."

"Okay."

"Sex was just how it was. I wasn't that evaluative. Think Wes wanted me to say how great *he* was or something. Maybe Wes had performance anxiety. Naturally, I *wanted* to be good in bed, but I didn't know one way or another. I certainly did not want him to think I was *frigid.*"

"Ouch."

I grimaced, "Yeah, yeah, really, that's what he said. He actually asked whether I was *frigid* or not."

Uncle R shook his head, "That's not cool. In fact, I think it's cruel. Wes was using mind manipulation to gaslight you. Really, you are better than that."

"Thanks, it's nice to know a shrink. Send me your bill. We're about an hour out of Amritsar, this is a special place." As she gave me a short shoulder rub, "Think you'll like it here."

I leaned back in the seat, and thought I'd close my eyes to rest for a moment.

Amritsar and the Golden Temple

The preeminent poet, Emily Dickinson (1830 – 1886), said,
"The soul should always stand ajar."

These are the days we were waiting for.

After my old friend Arthur's self-inflicted death, and adding in Shane Bighill's vegetative coma condition, as well as all the other goings on these days, when Raj suggested visiting the Golden Temple in Amritsar, I thought it would be a good idea. My previous two trips to India were whirlwind affairs where we went to several cities and famous sites, but they did not include the Golden Temple in Amritsar near the Pakistan border.

Back then it was repeatedly said, "Randal, we won't be able to see everything this trip." That was the mantra. "Next trip we will go north."

Okay, yet *"Go North Young Man,"* always sounded like the Canadian version of the United States manifest destiny mantra, but without adhering to the Americans' religious mission overtones. In the nineteenth century the United States settlers were told it was their *divine* destiny to remake the west into an agrarian society. The country needed some changes—go west and change the country. Continentalism and colonialism were hand in glove fitting concepts.

In the USA, masses of settlers sprang forth in caravan hordes screaming, "Westward ho." They hammered wooden stakes in the ground to show everyone that this was *their* land. Of course, that was news to the indigenous people who had lived there for many- generations. Soon the indigenous peoples unceded land was swallowed by settlers.

~

Historically, in psychology, the terms: *imbecile, idiot, moron,* and most recently, *retard,* were all once good clean clinical terms. No one got angry with any practicing shrink for using them. It was *normal.* Psychologists used them all the time. It was common practice. In fact, in British Columbia, right up until 2015 the government agency, Community Living BC, required a psychologist to document a person was *retarded* (IQ below 70) in order to receive government services. That's out of fashion, now. Autistic adults are harder to pigeonhole.

Similarly, nowadays I'm not using the term *stakeholder* anymore. It's out of fashion, too. Really, put a stake in the ground, to show it's your land, (but it isn't, really).

~

"Hey," something was poking me. "You awake with your eyes closed, or are you sleeping?" Parminder asked.

"Say again," I muttered, while taking the noise reducing ear-plugs out of my ears.

"We are here," she replied. "This is Amritsar."

Shaking off some slight grogginess and car confinement stupor, I said, "Great, what now?"

She smiled, "We will walk about a half kilometre to the Golden Temple's entrance. But first, you must take off those fancy shoes and no-see-them striped socks. You need to put on these flip flop sandals." She was waving a pair of black flip flops at me.

“Oh, no, thanks just the same,” I replied. “I’m crappy at walking in flip flop sandals. What’s wrong with my walking shoes?”

“Once we get inside, we go barefoot. The temple is the most holy of places we will ever set foot in. No shoes allowed.”

“Why’s that?”

Shaking her head Parminder explained, “Wearing shoes in the temple is a profanity. The ground is sacred.”

“Okay, good thing you are here to explain this stuff to me.”

With a smirky smile, “Ah, you’d learn fast enough. But, for sure, yes, I’m glad I’m here with you. Raj was right, this extended road trip is good for both of us. I enjoy explaining the mystery of the Punjabi history to you. It makes me think about all the religion my parents told me to take for granted. Teleologically speaking, its different seeing things from your angle. I’ve never known a licensed shrink before, just *unlicensed* kitchen shrinks. Get it?” She asked.

“Yes, I get it,” I said, nodding my head with a smile.

I was starting to grow fond of the various discussions with Parm, she’s a good kid. I’ve known her brother Raj, for forever. In the old days, the boys and I would sit around the campfire, or the burger joint booth, discussing the meaning of life, girls, and epistemology. Guess we’d chalk it up to *guy talk.* Parm, on the other hand, was different. Deeper discussions.

Tossing her hair behind her shoulder, Parm scrunched up her face and said, “All my life my parents have been indoctrinating their religious beliefs on me. Nowadays I am a little skeptical. Science suggests some of their religious notions and potions are kind of far-fetched, but I’m still trying to be respectful. After all, my mother taught me how to use a spoon. So, you know, she gets a wide margin. I know my matta ji loves me *unconditionally.* Whereas, my Pops, he has rules, stipulations, and conditions.”

"You think so?" I asked.

"I know so," Parm answering with a nod of firmness.

"Yes, parents, socialization, and religious indoctrination. As a child there is a level of susceptibility. At some point it becomes questionable."

"Well, science, evidence, and the supernatural oxymorons are more difficult with my advancing education and increased critical thinking," Parm suggested.

I grinned at her, "My father was an anthropologist at the U of Winnipeg."

Parminder's eyes lit up, "Wow, that's cool! An anthropologist, what does he say about religion?"

"He's been gone for a few years now." I told her about my childhood. "As an anthropologist, dad was a professional talker. He knew how to set a story, wade through the issues, and then bring it to a crescendo."

One story that stuck with me to this day was about the African pygmies in the Congo basin meeting missionaries. The pygmy people claimed that the river and the sun were their gods. However, the missionaries told them that was wrong. Their Christian god was the one *true* god. The pygmies didn't agree. "They killed the missionaries and ate them."

"Really." Parm was wide eyed and wondering.

I snorted, "Dunno, dad had lots of those types of anthropological stories. We heard many of them over and over again. He was my first teacher."

"Was he an atheist?"

"No, not really, but he wasn't agnostic neither. He looked at religion from an anthropological perspective."

"Yes, I guess I kinda understand," she nodded. "These things aren't binary or linear. Nothing is as simple as it seems."

"Agreed."

"Of course, I respect other people's religious practices," she held up a palm. "But most aren't my thing. Nevertheless, respect and reverence are important."

"Yes, anthropologically, dad reported it empirically interesting that almost every culture on the planet held some sort of supernatural belief system. He just didn't know which one was the preferred practice, or the *right* religion. Whenever someone from a different religious group was facing a tragedy, dad would say: "We may have different gods, but our prayers are the same."

David Bowie said, "Religion is for people who fear hell, spirituality is for people who have been there."

Parm ~ Quid Pro Quo

In 1955, Lewis Mumford (1895- 1990), the New York sociologist, said, "Adding car lanes to deal with traffic congestion is like loosening your belt to cure obesity."

Dearest Kelsey,

So, as I understand it, email is spotty in Puerto Rico, but surface mail works well. Go figure. Seems unusual to me, however, as our friend Edilma would say: let's test the theory. Thus, I am sending you a pen and paper longhand epistle. I am writing to you late at night from a hotel room in the middle of the Punjab.

Things are good with me—how about you?

I got your surface mail address from Ned Reilly. He had phoned my brother and asked if I had heard anything from you in Puerto Rico. Ned was the one who suggested a hard copy letter works better than email. He knows this stuff. Ned is constantly phoning my bro, Raj, to report on Shane Bighill (although there is never anything to report about his comatose condition) and check on the weather in India.

My brother Raj's brain has a phenomenal ability for mathematics and computers, yet nuclear family stuff leaves him short. He and his wife, Amelia, make a good pair. At first when they asked me to take Amelia's Uncle R on a road trip to Amritsar, of course, I emphatically said, "No." I've already spent too much time with the old guy.

Because Amelia is über pregnant Raj backed out of the commitment he made to our parents. He was expected to accompany me to auntie's Antam Sanskaar completion of life ceremony. Instead, they talked Uncle R into going as my travel companion.

Quid pro quo was Raj's explanation as to why I should take Uncle R to Amritsar to see the Golden Temple. "Parm, do this for me and I will owe you big time," Raj lamented. So, I relented. The notion of my bro owing me *big time* was appealing. Oh, and I should mention, they are compensating me quite well for my efforts. This is *easy money.*

Unlike small town Vancouver, everything in India is **old**. Traffic is terrible. I still remember the time you were bickering with Edilma about Vancouver's traffic, and the lack of adequate forward-thinking urban planning. You were the one who recited the American sociologist, Lewis Mumford's notion of giving a fat man a bigger belt is the same as adding more traffic lanes on the Oak Street Bridge.

While here in India, Amelia's Uncle R struggles with the noise from all the cars, and the traffic mayhem. He winces, saying, "This traffic, all these horns honking incessantly is nothing short of madness." The traffic cacophony is noisy, for sure. You don't get used to it or anything, you just deal with it. "Just the way it goes," I guess.

Earlier this morning I took him to visit the Golden Temple. He says his father was an academic anthropologist. Therefore, early socialization and family values shaped young Randy into someone who remains not religious, at all. Nevertheless, today he was quite moved by the whole temple experience. Now, I've been to the temple before, so I knew what to expect. It is a marvel even if you are not religious.

In addition to updated improvements to the Golden Temple's infrastructure, the city of Amritsar has put together some new plaques that commemorate the centenary of the 1919 Jallianwala Bagh massacre. This part of Punjab history just freaked him out massively. And this was even after my brother Raj tried to tell us, "You know the British did some *good* things for India. They built stuff and brought some common laws. India was not very modern, and the British tried to produce some progress to an ancient land."

Rightfully, as you would expect, Uncle R and I did a tag-team Vonnegutian slaughterhouse five attack, obliterating my bro Raj into oblivion, "WTF Raj, give your head a shake. Or smash it into the wall. Whatever, you are not thinking straight. You think *colonialism* was good?"

"Try and take a historical and broader perspective," Raj suggested.

"Jackass," was the best I could muster as a reply.

The Jallianwala Bagh massacre, also often referred to as the Amritsar massacre, took place on April 13, 1919. On that day well over a two thousand Sikhs had gathered at the seven-acre walled-in public garden park to celebrate the spring harvest known as Vaishakhi. This is on the same celebration scale as the Canadian Christmas.

The massacre started when Acting Brigadier-General Reginald Dyer wanted to show who was in control of the region. They blocked off the five exits to the Bagh. Then General Reggie ordered the British Indian Army troops to fire their rifles into the crowd of civilians. They murdered well over four hundred unarmed women, children, and men. Many others were seriously injured. Pure devastation and mayhem ensued. British colonialism run amok.

Today the British bullet holes are still evident in the walls. I took Uncle R to Bagh, which is now a park. The bullet holes in the wall were upsetting for him. "Wonder what makes Raj think colonialism contributed anything good for India?" he asked, while poking an index finger into the hole in the wall.

Took a while to calm Uncle R down. Ishan's colleague from college had us all over for dinner and they discussed colonialism, old India and neo-Indian politics. It was good. I'm not that politically inclined, but the food was fabulous. Nice people in Amritsar.

Tomorrow we leave to journey to the Taj Mahal. It's a love story, and a marvel of architecture. Did I mention my brother is paying me big bucks to serve as a tour guide? Actually, I'd likely do it for free, but I can use the dough.

So, dearest Kelsey, I should sign off now, put this missive in the mail, and get some sleep. More adventures tomorrow.

Take care, love and hugs,

Parminder

PS—I have called Caitlyn a bunch of times, but not connected. I did leave voicemail.

PSS—Did you ever see the movie Gandhi by Attenborough? I set it up for Uncle R to watch. Now I hear him making loud noises in the room next to me. I suspect he has messed up the feed. I'll go check on him. This is India.

Colonialisms

Mahatma Gandhi (October 2, 1869 – January 30, 1948) said,
"An eye for an eye will make the whole world blind."

This had been a busy day. Although my neuropsychological training and interpretive skills are not up to date, I can still remember Professor Jarman explaining why people on vacation get fatigued so quickly. Artie got it first crack.

"Okay, so you see Parm," I began to explain. "When someone from upcountry comes down to visit the big city, they get tired quicker than their normal rate of fatigue. Neurologists have experimented with lab rats and shown empirically how this works. Both auditory and visual stimuli produce similar results. Same thing with the field studies and follow up interviews."

At that point Parminder started making loud snoring sounds.

"Blarg," I muttered. "Are you messing with me, or are you really sleeping?"

Parm murmured something with a gurgling sound, and then she rolled over onto her side. Indeed, she was sound asleep, on the bed, in my hotel room.

"Guess we didn't need separate rooms," I said softly, with a smile.

We started out quite early this morning to visit the Golden Temple in Amritsar. It was ornate and amazing. There were throngs and throngs of people jostling for positions to get inside the temple. Getting out wasn't easy either. The Golden Temple is the most sacred and holiest place I had never set foot inside. However, afterwards, we visited the site where the Jallianwala Bagh massacre of 1919 occurred. That was overwhelming! Over a hundred years have lapsed and the British bullet holes were still in the walls where they murdered hundreds of innocent Sikhs. I found it all quite unsettling. Evidently, the massacre could have been *worse*. While the British were quick marching to the Jallianwala Bagh their combat tank with the machine gun turret got stuck in the narrow lane way. Brigadier-General Reginald Dyer had to proceed by foot.

When the troops entered the Bagh, a subordinate asked the general whether a warning to disperse should be issued. The general said no. He ordered the troops to commence shooting. It was a disgraceful massacre.

We discussed the British colonial history in India during dinner. Parm asked whether I had seen the classic 1982 Richard Attenborough movie about Gandhi. I said no hadn't heard about it.

"The film is well over three hours long, but it's an Academy Award winner. We can stream the movie from your cell phone to the big television screen in the hotel."

"My cell phone?"

"Yes, the cell phone Raj gave you. Easy-peasy, no problem, I'll show you how." Parm is a whizz with the tech things.

Shaking my head, I said, "Tech stuff is moving by me faster than I can keep up with all the changing innovations."

After a delightful, but heavy dinner, with a dozen different courses, we came back to the hotel. I adjourned to my room to watch the movie.

Sprawling out on the bed Parm pushes this and that button on the cell phone and then bingo bango the movie began playing. It started out with a bang, showing Gandhi's assassination in 1948. Then they jumped backwards to 1893 where a young twenty-three-year-old Gandhi is thrown off a South African train for sitting in the first-class compartment. Indians were not allowed there, despite the young Gandhi holding a first-class ticket. This marked the beginning of his nonviolent protest movement.

In 1915 Gandhi returned to India to help the movement to India's independence from the British Empire. The part in the film where they depict the Jallianwala Bagh massacre was quite unsettling for me. "They killed all those people in cold blood."

Parm held up a clenched fist and said, "That's the British for you."

It was a long film. I thought we were debriefing when Parm started snoring.

"Guess we didn't need separate rooms."

I reached over and turned out the lights.

"Gandhi was a good guy."

Sleeping Together

"Hi Raj, I slept with Uncle R last night. Other than that bit of news, I'm now trying to give you an update on our new revised travel plans but looks like I caught your voicemail. Or are you call screening? I'm using Uncle R's phone because mine doesn't have a royal data plan like his. Rich old white guys are mahjeeroms. Anyhow, long story made short, we are leaving this morning for Merhaj to go riding horses at Ruby's farm. Now I know what you are thinking — Parm doesn't know how to ride a horse. Precisely, that's what I said last night at dinner. However, Ishan's friend and Uncle R insist they can get me riding within ten minutes and within a couple hours I will feel confident as a beginner pro. So, I said okay. They were convincing. Besides, it's an adventure. Okay, adios for now. Bye. Oh, and you better call ma, but don't tell her I slept with Uncle R."

Under Pressure

Wayne Alfred Anderson (1950 – 2018) said,
"Don't feel like you are any under pressure, you aren't. Just get out there and do it."

I called Ned to talk. I needed to get his views on my situation. He's always been good at putting things in perspective. He has a wide-angle lens.

Oh great, got *his* voicemail, "Ned, answer your phone! It's me, Raj, calling. I've got to talk to you. I'm under a lot of pressure here. I'm calling back in ten minutes. So, answer when I call."

I waited five minutes and called him back. No answer, so I left him another voicemail.

"Oh, geez Ned, soon, like really soon, Amelia and I are having a *baby.* Well, she's giving birth, and I'm just the father. Whatever, I'm all stressed out, but pretending everything is cool. And to top things off, my stupid little sister was messing with my mind today. She leaves me voicemail saying she slept with Uncle R in Amritsar. I listened to her message and freaked out. Turns out she fell asleep on his bed watching a movie. She didn't really sleep with him in the sexual sense. But I didn't know that until I was able to track her down on the phone to scream at her that sleeping with a married man is totally wrong. She says I'm turning into our father and that makes me feel worse. I'm worried that I'm not going to be a competent father. My father and I have too much turbulence. I don't know. I'm all stressed out. The stuff with Shane has me unravelling. The coma thing is no good. Okay, I'm rambling. Maybe it's just jitters. Call me when you get this."

Sorrel Horses in India

"Don't let yesterday use up too much of today."
~Will Rogers (1879 – 1935)

Dusk was descending on the village of Mehraj, we were standing on the upper rooftop Juliette balcony watching as the farmhands released the sorrel horses to pasture for the evening. Turning to Parm who was standing beside me, "Those are nice horses, eh?"

"Yes, very majestic," Parminder smiled. "Those are beautiful horses."

I made a sweeping gesture, and asked, "So, are you happy? You learned how to ride a horse today."

"Yes, very much so. Thanks, that was so cool. My first time riding a horse. Loved it!"

Thinking back to my childhood, I was barely eight years old the first time I rode a horse. It was on my grandfather's farm in Southern Alberta. The horse was a large Clydesdale. A sorrel-coloured giant draught horse. Gramps explained that these work-horses were more reliable than the modern fancy farm machinery that was *always* breaking down. Whatever, who was I to argue? I was barely eight years old, from the big city, and only *visiting* the family farm under protest. This was all my mother's idea. "Randal, you are not going to spend all summer reading comic books and watching television in the basement. You are spending this summer on the farm with your grandfather."

Earlier that day my mother and I bickered about why she thought it was important for me to waste the summer on the old family farm. I thought it was a dumb idea and told her so in no uncertain terms.

Regardless of my feelings, and under protest, we left early in the morning to drive to the farm.

"Why do they have such rocky roads in the country? Why don't they have real roads like the city?"

"These are called gravel roads." She had the firm look of authority, holding the steering wheel firmly at ten and two o'clock hand positions. "Too expensive to pave country roads."

"Why do they put oil down on these gravel country roads?"

She seemed happy to discuss something other than my unhappiness. "They put oil on the roads to keep the dust down."

"Why, what's wrong with dust?" I asked.

"Too much dust makes the road unsafe. When two cars are traveling by each other in opposite directions too much dust makes it too hard to see. It's a safety thing."

"Dad's gonna be mad. You are getting the bottom side of the car awfully dirty with oil splashes."

"It's okay, I'll wash it when I get home?" said the expert washer woman.

"Dad says Gramps doesn't have electricity on the farm because he doesn't understand it."

That made her laugh, "Heh, who doesn't understand electricity, your father or grandfather?"

"Both of 'em."

"Your grandfather is a farmer. Your father is an academic anthropologist. They look a life differently." She shook her head and smiled.

"Okay, but Dad says, at nighttime Gramps lights the farmhouse with candles and oil lights."

"Yes, they are called kerosene lamps. They work well. He's been using them for years and years.

"I like electricity."

"Me too."

Finally, after what seemed like an eternity of boring country road driving, she made a sharp left turn onto the farm's old dirt road. No gravel now. Wow talk about a dusty driveway this one was rutted and rough. "Maybe we could slow down, eh," I asked while clutching the car seat door holder.

She just smiled and seemed to go faster. Finally, we stopped, "We're here," mum threw her arms in the air and seemed to shout with glee as nosed our way up to the farmhouse. Then she honked the horn *three* times. Normally, she curses horn honkers in the city.

"What are you doing? What's with honking the horn?"

She beamed with a big grin, "I'm letting Gramps know we're here. It's our arrival signal." She jumped out of the car, "C'mon, let's get your stuff and start unpacking."

We went inside the old farmhouse. "Whats the weird smell?"

She shrugged, "It's an old place, you'll get used to it."

"I don't think so."

She smiled insincerely, "You're going to sleep in my old bedroom."

"Okay."

We walked down the hall to the last room on the left. The bedroom was basic with a bed, dresser, chair, and not much more. A picture of mum hung on the wall. Out of the corner of my eye's peripheral vision, I saw something scurry by from underneath the bed, "What was that?" I asked with concern.

"What was what?"

Now I'm not usually squeamish or anything, but I looked under the bed and let out a yelp. "Yikes," I screamed.

My mother scoffed, "Relax, those are only mouse traps. No big deal, eh. It's a farm, got grains, and stuff. Mice are part of the place."

"There are two dead mice under the bed. What do you mean *no big deal?* Dead animals under the bed *is* a big deal. I'm not sleeping here!"

She was nonplussed, just kept unpacking my stuff. She finished, looked at me, and said, "Let's go have some lunch before I have to leave for home."

I like lunch.

We were sitting at the kitchen table, slurping soup, and nibbling on cheese sandwiches when I heard Gramps come clomping in through the porch door. My mum leapt up, "Hi Dad, are you hungry, I've got some lunch going."

"Of course, I'm hungry, it's lunchtime," he spoke gruffly.

I didn't know the farmhouse etiquette rules. Was I supposed to jump up from the table like mum? I was only eight years old and consequently enjoyed a margin of childhood not knowing stuff. So, I just sat there, raised my hand with a wave, and said, "Hi Grampa, the soup's good, and hot. Mum's a good cook."

Gramps was a big man, in oh so many ways. He filled the doorway and cast a large shadow. He washed his hands, sat at the head of the table, and waited for his lunch to be served.

"Were you in the barn?" mum asked while ladling soup into his bowl."

"Yep, dang tractor broke down again."

She shook her head in sympathy, "Which one broke down this time? The red one or green."

I thought to myself, "Two tractors, okay, this is cool!"

"The new one's not as reliable as ol' Bertha, but she's stronger."

Turns out Bertha was his favourite *old* tractor, reliable but not as powerful as the new one. I wondered whether Bertha was the red or green one.

My mum knew farm talk. I didn't. She could communicate with Gramps in a way that I didn't really understand, but I didn't care, either. "Any more soup?" I asked.

"Yes, I made plenty," she said with a smile, "you can have some with leftovers tomorrow."

Lunch came to a close. Gramps announced he had more work to do, and my mum said, "Okay, I better get going, too. Gotta get back to the big city before it gets dark."

Now I knew this was weird because its summer, darkness came late. She just wants to leave and now she was making up stuff.

"Alrighty, then," Gramps got up, "best be going."

We walked her to the car. She gave us each a hug. Then she threw some stuff in the trunk, got in and drove away. That was it. She was gone. Now it was just Gramps and me standing at the top of the driveway, waving goodbye to a trail of dust.

I didn't cry, just a watery eye. That's all.

Gramps started to shuffle off towards the barn, turned to me and asked, "You know how to ride a horse?"

"No."

"Wanna learn?"

"Sure."

"Let's go get you a horse to ride."

Gramps took big steps when he walks. I skipped along behind trying to keep up. As we started to approach the barn, I asked, "Whats that smell?"

"Barn smell."

"I don't understand."

"What don't you understand; why the barn smells or what?"

"Dunno," I shrugged, "Mum says she thinks it might take me some time to get used to this place and how farm life works."

"She said that."

"Yeah."

"Well, she should know. This was where she was born and raised."

"That's what she said, too. And then she said I'm not supposed to talk to you about Grandma."

"Whys that."

"Cuz Grandma's dead and talking about her makes you sad and mad."

"Suppose that's true, I still miss the old girl. Wish she were here."

"So that's the sad part. Mum says the mad part is the cancer thing."

"What?" he shook his head. "No sense getting made at the cancer. It doesn't matter. Cancer don't care."

We walked through the barn while he grabbed some leather strap things along the way to the horses in the field on the other end of the barn.

"What do you do with those?" I asked.

"These are called the bridle, bit, and reins. You need them to ride the horse."

I gave him another shrug, "Okay."

Then, suddenly, Gramps makes a weird whistling sound and a giant reddish colour horse comes out from the trees trotting towards us. "This is Rena," he said, as he patted her giant neck. "She's a good old girl. You can ride her easy like. She's called a Clydesdale. She's a working horse."

"Okay," I was a bit nervous now, but excited, too. "Don't I need the seat-thing put on her?"

"Nope," he was putting the bridle and reins on her, "bare back's the best way to learn. You don't need a saddle."

"Okay."

"You ready."

"Guess so."

He picked me up and heaved me way up high onto the giant Clydesdale horse's back. He handed me the reins, gave a me a quick two-minute lesson on steering the horse. "You go ahead and take her for a ride. I'll be in the barn working on the tractor. Holler if you need me."

"Okay," I nodded. "How do I get down? I can't jump off her from this height without committing suicide."

He scowled, "That's right, don't jump, she wouldn't like that. Just go over to the corral fence and climb down or ride over to the barn and get me. But why the hell you talking about getting down already? You just got on her."

"Dunno," I said softly, "just planning ahead, I guess. Reilly's are like that, right?"

He muttered something low, started walking away, turned, and said, "Rena's a good horse. You'll have a nice ride with her. Don't kick her like you see assholes on television. She doesn't like stupid stuff."

And that was that. Rena and I started to tour all around the farm. I held the reins tight, tried some steering stuff, but she just sorta walked around wherever she wanted. Sometimes she'd bend her head down to eat grass. That freaked me out first time. Mostly we strolled around the farm fields. It was terrific. I was horseback riding! It was a wonderful afternoon, but getting on to late afternoon, I guess. The time goes fast when you are having fun.

Suddenly, she stopped in her tracks. From some distance Gramps had made that same weird whistle sound. Rena heard it, turned around and trotted back to the barn. I knew this meant something, but I didn't know what it meant other than to hold her hairy mane and reins a little tighter. I didn't want to fall off.

Gramps was walking around doing chores or something. When we got closer, I yelled, "Hey Gramps, we're here."

"Hi Randy," he waved. "I see that. Did you have a good ride?"

"Yes, just great." I gently patted Rena. "She's the best horse ever."

I leapt off Rena into Gramps waiting arms. We started putting stuff away, because those are the farm rules. I was learning, there are a lot of farm rules. I'm discovering more of them as we roll along. "You always put stuff away."

"You getting hungry," Gramps asked.

"Sure," I smiled, "I'm always hungry."

"You like chicken dinner?"

Seemed early to start thinking about dinner, guess my family eats later than farm folks. Dad often stays late at the university. Traffic or something, I dunno, "Yeah, sure, chicken dinner sounds like a good idea," I said, still feeling the glow from horseback riding all afternoon. I was in a good mood.

"Let's go to the chicken coop and get a couple birds for dinner."

He lumbered along and I skipped behind, not really able to keep up with his strides. The chicken coop was another weird building on the other side of the barn where the horses were kept. It was stinky. Different stinky than the barn, but stinky.

On the drive down to the farm my mum had warned me that Gramps would likely expect me to do *chores* around the place. "No one gets a free ride on the farm."

Gathering eggs would likely be one of those chores. What was I to say other than, "Okay, I guess?" Chores weren't part of my city repertoire, but whatever, I didn't care because where I come from, we "*go along to get along.*"

Gramps grabbed two chickens, muttered, "Follow me."

I didn't know what was going on or anything. I'm eight years old. All this farm stuff was quite unusual for me. However, when he took a hatchet, cut the heads off the chickens, and they ran around like chickens with their heads cut off, I completely lost it, freaked out, and started screaming. "Holy crap-olie," as the blood spurted and gushed out everywhere.

I ran back to the farmhouse. Went to the wall where there was an old-fashioned telephone. I dialed my mum's number. Panicking and talking to myself, "I'm not staying here, I am not staying here. Gramps is crazy." Of course, no one was home. No one answered the telephone. I sat down and cried on the floor of the kitchen hallway.

Counting to one hundred often calms me down according to my mum. I counted to one hundred, twice, and then dialed the number again. Fortunately, or not, as it may be, my father answered. He's an anthropologist. I explained my situation the best I could. He explained farm life the best he could. It was no use talking to him. So, he put my mum on the line. She made things worse by asking whether Gramps had asked me to help "*pluck feathers* from the birds by hand because he didn't use a machine for feather removal!"

The long and the short of the situation was clear. I was stuck here. No one was coming to get me. This is how it is on the farm.

Gramps eventually came clomping in through the door. He asked if I was okay, which was nice. He said *sorry* if butchering chickens upset me. He forgot I was a *city kid* and maybe didn't understand farm life.

"You want pancakes and berries for dinner?" Gramps asked.

"Yeah, sure, I like pancakes for dinner."

"You wanna ride the same horse tomorrow, or a different one?"

"Same horse," I replied. "I like Rena. She's a good horse."

"Okay, we'll do that tomorrow."

-~-

Parminder gave me a soft poke in the ribs, "You look lost in thought."

I snapped out of my daydream, smiled, "Yes, I was remembering the first time I rode a horse."

"Cool," she said, "let's go get some of Ruby's homemade ice cream and you can tell us all about it."

-~-

"Clydesdales are good horses." ~Martin Julson (1891 – 1967)

Life Expectancy

"People be patient please. This is going to take a minute or two to figure out."
~Don Lanyon (1929 – 2020)

Raj and I have been discussing *possible* baby names. Raj knows the *successful* name will not be achieved via rock-paper-scissors decision making methodology. Nevertheless, we have certainly started talking about possible candidate baby names, and although there is no immediate urgency, the discussion is underway and developing. I'm thinking girl names. He's suggesting a boy.

Previously, we purposely decided to not ask the obstetrician about gender. "I can tell you, if you'd like to know," she said.

"No, it'll be a surprise," I replied. However, I'm now thinking next ultrasound scan I might peek at the screen. The current suspense overrides the pregnancy induced anxiety. I'm thinking we should reduce the variables that are in play and learn the gender. Raj is romantically idealistic about it all. Meanwhile, I'm über pregnantly hormonal, bio-chemically compromised, and worried about bringing a baby into this world at this time in world history. Raj, cool as a cucumber, says, "Don't worry, it'll all work out just fine. Trust me."

"Okay, in this world, more than anyone, Raj, in you I trust."

My grandfather was an anthropologist from the University of Calgary. Then he got promoted to the University of Winnipeg. I've been thinking about him a lot lately. I miss him. He died at age eighty-eight. Although his death was not expected, it wasn't unexpected, either. Eighty-eight is old.

Gramps always said, "Something is going to get all of us some time. We don't know the *thing* and we don't know the *time,* but it's a fact of life. We are all going to die sooner or later. Of course, the later the better because I have a book to finish."

Gramps didn't finish his last book, he died in his sleep. He went to bed one night and didn't wake up the next morning. My brother Ned said he thought that was a good way to go. "We don't like violent deaths. They're the worst."

For a little while, I spent too much time spinning stuff around my head, perseverating over the Congo Pygmies, and my grandfather's death. He spent a good portion of his academic life as an anthropological Pygmy scholar. I remembered reading in one of his early books where Gramps analyzed and described at great length how Pygmies often died in their sleep. "That's an empirical fact, a counting census. No opinion or analysis needed. A significant number of pygmies die during sleep."

I was twelve years old the first time I read Gramps' monograph about the Congo Basin Pygmies. By that age my reading comprehension had improved immensely. I started 'reading' at age three, but Gramps argued with my mum that I was only "barking at words," and not really reading. Comprehension, synthesis and application was what Gramps valued. "That's real reading!"

My mum, and all the reading coaches she had on tutorial retainers, taught me how to decode words from flash cards and PowerPoints. Nevertheless, Gramps was correct I wasn't *really* reading. Developmentally, from a Piagetian perspective, I wasn't there, yet. Of course, mum argued her case vehemently. "Decoding precedes comprehension."

Although starting at age three they also taught me how to identify artists' paintings from flash cards and power point slides, any art appreciation claims were far-fetched. I was *three* turning *four*. However, I could correctly identify a Claude Monet painting, a Pablo Picasso, a Paul Cézanne, a Vincent van Gogh, a Henri Matisse, and all the Canadian Group of Seven Artists. Gramps acknowledged, "That's nice Annette, but means *nothing*. A child walks and talks when they are physically and neurologically *ready*. This process can't be purchased or speeded up."

Gramps was correct and my helicopter hovering mother missed the meaning of the concept. Art appreciation and the fact that beauty lies in the eyes of the beholder are hard to get a net over and reel into the boat. "It's art."

I'll still fondly remember Gramps showing me some of his African photography collection. He had pics from his early anthropology fieldwork researcher days. Gramps looked so cool posing for pictures with Pygmies. He pointed out the hole in the roof of the Pygmy hut. "Pygmies always have a hole in the roof of their huts. They need the hole so their spirit can wander while sleeping and dreaming. Pygmies believed that they would die in their sleep if they were hunting during a dream and a wild animal killed them. They must have the hole in the roof in order get back into their body, otherwise they'd die."

Sometimes I slip and start to obsess too much about stupid stuff. I know it's just an overthinking problem, but I can't seem to avoid the spinning brain cells over and over. Pedestrian stuff is the worst. Yet the idea of gramps dying in his sleep makes me think about the Pygmy huts with a hole in the roof. Wonder what gramps was dreaming about when his heart stopped?

Gramps taught me about quantity *and* quality of life. I was thirteen years old when he called me up saying, "I need a research assistant. It's time you started doing some research work."

"Sure."

At first Mother, of course, mitigated the magnitude of this research assistant position making like it was just a convenient method for Gramps to send some money my way. That was not true, far from it.

"This is no sinecure, Amelia. I'm expecting some strong work from you on this project," Gramps said with an emphatic tone.

"Yes, for sure," I told him, "I won't let you down. Let's get started."

Previously, Gramps had been involved with the shutting down of the old Woodlands School (institution) in Vancouver. He said it was nothing more than a human warehouse for children with developmental disorders. Took from 1887 to 1996 to get the place closed down for good. Originally, it was called the *British* Columbia *Provincial Lunatic Asylum.* In 1950 the new name was Woodlands School, but Gramps said it was just a name change. It was where institutionalizations of all sorts of people persisted.

"Everyone knows children should live with their families in their own neighbourhood. Normalization not warehousing was the goal. Institutional is *wrong.*"

Gramps was writing a new book on the anthropological cross-cultural perspectives towards Downs Syndrome. He hired me to do some library research at first. Then he had me doing telephone and field work in-person structured interviews with focus group families. It was good work.

I got paid, what I considered a tonne of crisp cash from his Canada Social Science Research fund, and additionally, maybe more importantly, I got written published credits in the foreword, footnotes, and acknowledgment sections of the book. And, to top it all off, Gramps said, "I'm proud of you, Amelia. You did some good work on this project."

Prior to this project I knew nothing about John Langdon Down, the British scientist who first described the etiology and causes of the syndrome in 1866. During the two years I worked as Gramps research assistant I became an '*expert*' in the area. Yet, more significantly, I became an advocate. I could talk at length, to anyone I could get to listen, about how Down's Syndrome people are living longer.

Thus, an increase in the *quantity of life*. However, *quality of life,* is also accelerating. Of course, as a society, we have a long way yet to travel down this road but remember "Rome wasn't built in a day."

"Thanks Gramps."

Just a little over ten years after the completion of our Downs project, I earned a law degree and a medical degree, concurrently, from UBC. I wanted the best of both disciplines. In the beginning it wasn't easy dealing with all their institutional bureaucracy, but at the time it certainly seemed as though it was worth it. Self-advocacy and tough negotiating got the door open. The rest was history.

Nowadays, I don't know. Shane's situation has put me off the law for a while.

Gramps got me into research work all those years ago. It suits me well now that I'm über pregnant. Of course, I can't quit wondering whether I might have a Downs Syndrome baby. After all, I'm almost thirty-three. I've spoken to Raj about it, but he just scoffs and says I know too much and need to relax. "Don't overthink this," Raj said encouragingly. "Don't go looking or inventing problems."

"Okay, I'll try to not think about the mathematics of a thirty-three-year-old woman and Down's Syndrome, but you're the one who introduced me to the Punjabi saying: *easy to say, hard to do.*"

Raj smiled, shook his head, put his hands in the air to surrender, and then he walked out of the room.

Guess I did not need to tell him that if I deliver a Downs baby, I'm fine with that. Whatever, this baby is a gift.

"Hope he or she is right-handed. Lefties are nothing but trouble,"

I yelled down the hall.

Raj said something back to me in Punjabi. I couldn't hear him clearly, so I just let it slide. These are the dance steps we're doing these days.

"If babies born in 2020 live eighty years, they will see the year 3000. Wonder how long this baby I am carry will live?"

Smiling to myself I thought about Gramps. He said, "Amelia, you should not confuse life expectancy with life's experiences. Don't sit on the shore watching the river flow by, get out there and swim."

"Thanks Gramps," I sighed. "Time to start swimming. If tomorrow is the first day of the rest of my life, I'd better get started."

A Grandmother

"Resentment is like drinking poison and waiting for the other person to die."
~John Dickerson

"So, Ned, your Uncle Randal sends an email informing me that I am going to be a *grandmother* in short order. Not a word from your sister as to where or when. How do you think I should react?"

Ned stands, smiles, hugs me hard, and says, "Mum, you should be crazy happy. This is good news, it's a big deal! C'mon, we're celebrating. You are going to be a *grandma!*"

And that's all it took for me to realize perspective is everything. Ned knows how to re-frame things so I can understand easier. Don't know why I get caught in the smaller details.

"Yes, let's celebrate."

When I think back sometimes it seems like Amelia and I have been battling since her birth. Eighteen hours of hard hospital labour, and there she was — out, and yelling at me from her first moments on earth.

Of course, her father, Thomas, saw it differently, he said, "She's singing!" Thomas has *never* been much help with *anything.* He's a musician.

Amelia and Thomas always had music as a common denominator. Together they could sing, compose, theorize, accompany each other, and *feel* the music. I was always on the opposite end of the spectrum. Boringly, I had household rules for *everyone* to follow. Both of them disliked my household rules. "Creative cooking is fine, but you two must clean up the mess." Then they look at me quizzically.

"Who me?"

After our divorce Thomas spent more and more time as a traveling musician on the road. Eventually, he his band, The *Mahjeeroms*, made it to a certain level of mediocre celebrity standing. Thomas started making money. That was nice, I didn't have to pay palimony support payments. As a father, Thomas was pretty, much absent, but his absence didn't seem to bother Amelia or Ned. My brother, Randal, was always around if they needed a father figure. "Uncle R will know the answer."

Nobody offers a mother much sympathy for the difficulties involved with raising a gifted girl. "Amelia speaks *five* languages?" Asked the neighbour.

"Yes, and can argue in a half dozen."

"Six?"

"Yes, nonverbal willfulness is her sixth language."

Amelia excelled at school. Everyone could see she was bright. I was always *trying* to balance her academic exploits with what I thought to be a well-rounded education. I didn't want her to grow up too fast. But, often, simply seemed as though I was blocking her path. She could argue, and cross examine better than most. What I thought was right, she thought contrary, but she insisted she was not a contrarian.

When Amelia decided she wanted to earn a law degree and medical degree concurrently, I tried to dissuade her. The University of British Columbia admissions officials also tried to dissuade her, at first. However, when Amelia persisted, started receiving acceptance notifications from other prestigious universities with money, UBC caved. Amelia told them that they must "meet or beat" the other universities offers, or she would go elsewhere. "The University of Montreal has made a generous offer."

Finally, Amelia secured some scholarships, special funding, and in the end decided to stay in Vancouver, stick with UBC, and live at home—for a while. I was pleased in the sense that it was better to have her stay in town. I didn't want her moving to Quebec, NYC, or Los Angeles. "Money isn't everything."

I liked the idea of Amelia following my footsteps earning a law degree. I became a lawyer to change the world. Of course, she disputed this saying, "Mum, it's okay, everyone knows you went into law to make *money*. You could have become a scholar like your father."

"Amelia, that's not true!"

"It is, and that's okay. You are you."

I was flummoxed. Amelia could do that to me. So, I ended up retorting with, "Actually, your grandfather would disagree. I've made some important contributions to the legal community."

"Are you *kidding* me, who do you think first told me that you became a lawyer to make money?"

"Who?"

"Gramps, that's who."

Arguing with Amelia was senseless. When I asked why she needed both a law and medical degree, she simply said it was a no brainer. Medicine is the first science. She loves science. Legal training was necessary to enforce medical principles. The rule of law needs science to develop.

And so it was, Amelia was an excellent student. She graduated with flying colours. She passed the bar exam, secured a medical practice license, and opened a laboratory at UBC.

We always had what my brother called mother/daughter conflicts and collisions. "You two are always butting heads like a bull moose battle."

Shane Bighill's parents died in a car accident when Shane was eighteen years old. Consequently, because Shane is my son's best friend, over the years, I have always tried to help as much as possible when Shane needed legal assistance. And he often required a lawyer for the various scrapes and run-ins with regulatory authorities, and the police. However, it all came crashing to a crescendo when Shane was charged with murdering two young men.

Amelia and I served as co-counsel on the case. The crown prosecutor originally charged Shane with second degree murder. The evidence was not in Shane's favour. There were eyewitnesses who would testify that they saw Shane kill the men, and CCTV video footage of the murder.

Amelia was adamant that we should go to trial and claim self defence. I disagreed. Rolling the dice with a jury given the evidence against Shane did not seem wise. I negotiated a plea bargain deal for manslaughter. Shane received a prison sentence of four years.

That was the beginning of the end for Amelia and me.

Ned moved in with Nina the day Shane was sentenced to prison. Amelia went to India for a couple weeks, came home in a mood, and then she and Raj got married on the deck of my brother's cottage on Mayne Island. She was mad at me about Shane's conviction. Amelia probably had no intention of inviting me to the wedding, but it was at my brother, Randal's place, and he more or less made sure I attended. I carpooled with his wife, Harjit.

Of course, as I understand it, Amelia didn't actually *want* to get married, however, Raj said that marriage was the *only* way they could live together in India. "It's an old-fashioned country."

And now she's pregnant, Amelia is going to have a baby soon. I'm going to be a *grandmother!*

I thought about it for a minute or so. As we speak, my brother is currently touring all over India with Raj's younger sister, doing God knows what. My daughter, whether she knows it or not, needs me! I'm her mother. I'm the baby's *grandmother.*

"Ned, pack your suitcase. We're going to India."

Part Six

SHANE'S COMA

Nina Simone (1933 – 2003) sang,
"They say everything can be replaced.
They say every distance is not near, So I
remember every face, Of every man who put
me here." ~ *I Shall Be Released*

Hello Old Friend

Daniel Fogelberg (1951- 2007) sang,
"The audience was heavenly, but the travelling was hell."
~*Same Old Lang Syne*

"Hello Shane," said the angel dressed in blue at the end of my bed.

"How are you feeling today?"

"You are a nurse, right?" I asked.

"Yes," she pointed to her name tag, "I'm Diana Donnelly. You can call me DD."

"Okay."

I explained to DD that some things are clear, some things are blurry, I remember some stuff, kinda, yet it's random. I don't really know what's going on. "Why am I here, and how did I get here?"

Nurse DD explained that I am in the Vancouver General Hospital. I've been in a coma for *seven months.* And now I'm not. Guess I'm back to the land of the living, but from wherever, I'm messed up in many ways. I am quite confused.

Shortly thereafter talking with DD all these doctors, nurses, and physiotherapists start to come in the room. They begin by poking and prodding me. The shrinks and neurologists ask *lots* of questions, most of which I can't answer. Then they move to the back of the room whispering words I cannot not decipher. People come and people leave the room. I can't walk because of muscle deterioration, atrophy, and the applied bio-mechanical principle of: *if you don't use it you lose it.*

My twin sister, Nina, who I didn't really recognize her at first, but I pretended I knew who she was. Just didn't know her name, however, didn't know *my* own name either, at first.

"How can you be my twin? You are a girl with black hair. I got red hair?"

Nina smiled, "Well, we are sororal twins. We aren't identical, we are fraternal twins."

"Same sorority, eh?"

"Yes, technically, from the same genetic endowment, but we didn't share the same placenta. You had your own placenta. We shared the womb."

"Where are our parents?"

A tear came to her eye. "You don't *remember* our parents?"

"No, sorry, I don't remember much of anything, but those nice ladies who left just when you arrived say they *expect* I will start to remember stuff sometime soon. The Asian woman says she is an applied clinical neurologist. The Irish lady is nurse DD. They are helping me figure stuff out."

"Well, that's good. Getting your memory back is a big recovery step."

"So where are our parents?"

"Our mum and dad died in a car accident a nine years ago."

"Ouch, a car accident. Guess that's why they aren't here, eh?"

"Yes, yet I always sorta feel as though they are here with us. Mum sits on my shoulder like a homunculus."

"That's cool, does she have red hair?"

"Not really, mum was a strawberry blonde."

"Father?"

"What about father? What's your question?"

"Red hair?"

"No, black."

"Who's the guy with curly hair that comes and stands at the back of the room and cries? He's not a doctor."

"Correct, he's not a doctor. That's Logan Myers, he's one of your friends from childhood. You don't remember *him*?"

"No, right now I don't remember very much of anything, let alone my childhood. What's with him crying?"

"Well, Logan has always been high strung. He's been coming to see you in the hospital every day since Mrs. Reilly got you transferred here from the Saskatchewan prison hospital. Often, he comes late at night by himself and sings you songs. Sometimes he brings his four-year-old daughter, Banny. She climbs all over your bed and tells you what is going on in her life. Sometimes Logan brings his dad. His mother has come here, too. The Meyers are divorced, and they can't all come at the same time."

All this boggled my mixed-up mind! "So why is he sad? Crying"

"He's not sad," Nina said while scrounging her face. "Logan was the first person here when you came out of the coma the first time, but you didn't know who he was."

"First time?"

"Yes, you have been in and out of the coma a few times. The last time you came out of the coma was three days ago. Then you slipped back in for another couple of days. Logan's probably worried that this period won't last."

"What won't last?"

"Your current consciousness levels. They say you may slide back into an unconscious state again. The doctors told me there is a strong likelihood you might relapse more than once."

"Transferred from the Saskatchewan prison hospital, and who's Mrs. Reilly?"

"Annette Reilly is your friend Ned's mother. She's a lawyer."

"Okay, who is Ned, and why was I in a Saskatchewan prison hospital?"

Nurse DD had come back into the room and had been standing off to the side, "Very well then," she came over to the bedside and started messing with the tubes stuck in my arm, "think that's likely enough visiting for now. Shane needs to rest because we are wheeling him down to the MRI clinic as soon as we get a green light opening. We can do more questions later."

Nina smiled, nodding her head in agreement, "Yes, thanks DD." She kissed me on my forehead. "I'll see you later Shane. Be good."

"Okay," but I thought what does *that mean*? Be good. Guess it would be weirder if she said, be bad. Dunno, but this is all awfully mind boggling. "Before you go, why was I in a *prison*. What did I do?"

Nina came back to the bedside, stroked my hair, "Don't worry about it. It's complicated. You are here now. I'll explain everything later. It's going to take some time I suspect."

Nurse DD patted Nina on the shoulder and said, "The sedative should settle Shane for now. We don't want him getting too excited before the next MRI."

Nina seemed to agree, "Yes, thanks DD."

Then everything went blurry to brown to down. I was out of it.

David Gill Reilly was Born

"Life is the sum of all your choices."
~Albert Camus (1913 – 1960)

After *eight* hours of labour, February 11, 2020, early Tuesday morning at 6:42, David Gill Reilly was born in the Chandigarh Silver Oaks Hospital, weighing in at 7 lbs. and 12 ounces (3.51 kilos). I had delivered healthy boy. Ten fingers, ten toes, and a sweet little nose.

David was the final first name Raj and I could agree on together as *acceptable.* We had already bickered too much on the surname selection order. When we married, I kept my maiden name: *Reilly.* Mostly because all my documents, university degrees, driver's license, passport and whatnots were listed under the name Reilly. I simply did not want to expend the energy to change all those things. It was not a political feminist statement, I was not snubbing the Gill name, or anything of such. I wasn't motivated to do the work to change my surname. Reilly is the name I am used to, why change now.

Truth be told, I didn't want to get married in the first place. We got married because Raj insisted that was the only way we could live together in India, peacefully. And I wanted to live with Raj.

I love the Sikhs. It's a beautiful religion, as far as religions go. However, I am *not* a Sikh, and I am not religious neither. The Catholics can get crazy, but don't get me started.

Traditionally, a male Sikh has the middle name of Singh. Female Sikhs middle name is Kaur. The first name is generic. Both males and females can be called Rajinder. There are several Rajinders in the neighbourhood where we live in Chandigarh. Of course, there's only one Raj for me, but we had to bicker a bit about David's middle name. In the end we *compromised.*

We knew we were going to have a boy because the ultrasound picture showed us a penis. So, we *started* discussing names during the third trimester. In the end we agreed the baby's birth certificate would say David *not* Davindar. No middle name needed. *Two* surnames, no hyphen: *David Gill Reilly.*

We couldn't call him Reilly Gill because both of us thought that sounded silly. The phonemes weren't there for that. Thus, the joint surname Gill Reilly was settled. The bases were covered.

Raj suspected some of this might be hard to sell to his family. Afterall, they didn't *know* I had *kept* my *maiden* name. The English language is stupid enough. Some of the customs are dumber. My grandfather was an anthropologist. He understood cultures for a living. I wish he was here.

So, good luck Raj. My family, on the other hand, had fallen off the Richter Scale of happiness. They all showed up here in India for David's birth. We agreed *only* Raj was allowed in the delivery room, thank goodness. Otherwise, my mother, my brother, and Uncle R all kept vigil awaiting the baby's birth. Auntie Harjit had a court case and couldn't come. I'm sure she was relieved to be excused. I was wishing to find an excuse to not be here many times after my family had descended upon our house. It was more than I anticipated. Too many personalities with family history.

My mother and brother were *not* invited by Raj or me. My mother invited *herself* and made Ned tag along for company, and to carry all her bags. Yet, all in all, it was good. More or less, it was generally okay. Everyone was happy. Raj was ecstatic to see my brother, Ned. They are childhood friends.

That was one thing, then Raj's family descended upon us. Parminder takes responsibility for bringing them.

Raj's mother could not stop crying. She was too happy to breathe. Once or twice, I saw Raj and his father holding an amicable conversation. Historically, that *seldom* happens.

Truthfully, David is *beautiful.* He is a heart-melter. He's so soft, smells good, and represents the miracle that childbirth is all about. Nevertheless, I wish some of these idiots would stop asking if *we* are going to have another kid straight away or wait a while. "There's no *we* in our pregnancy or childbirth—it's me! Raj tries to be helpful, but he has too many limitations to list."

I know my mother likely started that scenario. That's the type of thing she'd do. Another kid?

Finding My Way Back Home

"It is an ironic habit of human beings to run faster when
we have lost our way."
~Rollo May (1909 – 1994)

My sister Nina has been nothing but helpful. I have been pretty messed up. My mind has spun about needlessly in strange directions. Maybe thanks to the drugs? Nina seems to know what's going on. I'm kinda fuzzy on the whole thing.

Nurse DD says, "We have to get you up and walking soon, Shane."

Walking, on my own steam, well, that might take some time, I guess. The wheelchair is nice. The physiotherapist is kinda pushy, but I understand what she's trying to achieve. No pain, no gain.

Logan, who claims to be *my best friend,* brought in a bunch of high-tech electronics for me to use. We musta been really good friends because this level of dedication is really something else altogether. These gadgets are awesome, but the learning curve is so steep.

"So, Shane," Logan starts to explain, "this new phone iteration, the tablet and laptop are all synched together. You can use whichever one suits your situation. Nurse DD and all these other medical guys are saying we must work on your communication skills because they are correlated to cognitive recovery. You gotta start talking to people, asking questions and listening. You gotta figure things out."

"Figure out what? What sort of questions?" I asked.

"Dunno," he shrugged. "I'm just following through on the séance we had yesterday in the conference room."

"Séance?"

"Yeah, séance, I got that from Ned. That's what he would call those early morning meetings in the conference room where they would *update* us on your prognosis, diagnosis and med stats situation. Your sister, Nina, *liked* those conference room meetings. So, don't bring it up."

"Okay, I won't"

Logan waves this phone type device in my face. "Alright, pay attention pal, here's how this works. What's your favourite colour?"

"My favourite colour?"

"Yeah, what's your favourite colour?" Logan asked again.

"I think I like all the colours the same," I replied.

"No, no, you don't," Logan shakes his head. "Blue, that's your favourite colour. Blue!"

"Okay, if you say so."

"Yeah, see this blue button, that's me. You push this blue button or the number 1 because I *am number one* and you will get me. Anytime, day or night, you push blue and you got me. Now, maybe I might be in the shower or with Wendy or something, you just leave a message, and I will get back to you straight away. Okay, you got that?"

"Yes."

"Okay, green, that's your sister, Nina. Push the green button or number 2 and you will get Nina. Green is good. You got that?"

"Yes, I think so." I tried to reassure Logan because he seemed quite intense about this stuff. "Green is good."

"Red is Ned," he kept going on with colours and buttons.

"Where is Ned?" I asked.

"He's in India. His sister just had a baby boy. Shane, we are *uncles!*"

"We are," now I really didn't know what he was on about, but Logan seems so happy that I couldn't spoil the mood. He says we are uncles. Guess that's gotta be good.

"Try it," he implored me, "push a button."

"Which one?"

"Any one, you choose."

I pointed to the yellow button, "This one?"

"Sure," Logan smiled, "yellow is my dad, Gerry. You remember my dad, right?"

"No, not really."

"That's okay, don't worry about."

I felt confused and overwhelmed, "Logan, how I am going to remember any of this. It all seems a bit complicated."

"Cheat sheet!" he replied with delight and gusto. "We have a cheat sheet developed specifically for you. It's easy-peasy."

"Cheat sheet?"

"Yeah, yes, look here, the tablet is a good way to go, but the phone and laptop will work just fine, too. So, you tap or click on a button and then that person's picture, their numbers, and who they are to you shows up here."

"Okay." I was impressed.

"Watch this," he pushed the green button and Nina's picture came out. Then the machine's sound voice said, "Shane this in Nina Bighill, she is your fraternal twin sister." Then the thing started ringing.

"Alright," Logan smiled, "we're calling Nina. Say, hello, when she picks up."

She didn't pick up. After three rings her thing said, "Hello, this is Dr. Nina Bighill, please leave a message and I will return your call."

Logan leaned over, "Hi Nina, it's Logan and Shane. We are trying out his new tech devices. Call us when you can. Catch you later."

He raised his palms, "Sometimes people are busy, so leave them a message. I guarantee they will be happy to hear from you. Short messages are good, don't ramble on with a long message."

"Okay."

"Here," he grabbed the thing from my hand, "push the white button, that's Nurse DD. See there is her picture. It reads Nurse DD is Shane's favourite nurse, an angel in white. Get it?"

"No, I don't get it."

"Yeah, yeah, I programmed it that way. Nurse DD's pic appears, and it lets you know who she is to you. Get it?"

"Yes, I guess."

"Oh, it's ringing her number."

"Hello, is that you Shane?" Nurse DD asked.

"Yes," Logan yelled at her, "we are working with the new equipment."

"Very well," she replied, "I am just down the hall. Do you need me?"

"No," I answered, "we are good. Logan is teaching me how to use the new stuff."

"Very well then, glad to hear that Shane. You can call me *any time* you want, day or night." Nurse DD hung up saying, "See you later."

"Okay, thanks Nurse DD."

Logan seemed awfully happy that the equipment was working for me.

"See, the *cheat sheet* is good, eh?"

"Yes, it is helpful." I nodded my head in appreciation.

"Who do you want to call now?" he asked.

"No one," I yawned, "I think I need a nap. I'm tired."

"Yeah, yeah, that's cool. I gotta get home anyhow. Call me later Shane?"

"Okay."

"You promise."

"Yes."

"What's my button's colour?"

"Blue, because Logan is number one."

"That's right buddy."

Logan kissed me on my forehead and took off in a whirlwind.

I was rapidly drifting off to sleep, remembered the green button for my fraternal twin sister, Nina. Green is good. Her button said leave a message for Dr. Nina, and she'll call back.

I didn't know my sister is a doctor. She didn't mention that. That's nice. Wonder what kind of doctor? Gotta remember to ask her about it. Tomorrow…

Onwardly Optimistic

"Seattle's King County Prison is a rough place to be forced inside, especially when you know it is *wrong*."
~Gordon K. Hirabayashi (1918 – 2012)

The same day Shane was put in prison Ned moved in with me. We had been together for a while. Unilaterally, Ned moved the needle to the next level. We officially started living together. It was good. I needed his help, but tried to deny it, at first. We have not been apart since then. However, when his mother asked Ned to accompany her on a trip to India for the birth of his new niece it was a *no-brainer,* "Ned, there's *nothing* to discuss. Your sister is having a *baby*. Your mother needs you to go with her. So, go!" I told him.

"Yes, Nina," Ned seemed as though he wanted to discuss or debate the merits of the trip, but he thought twice when I gave him the furrowed brow look, "I guess you are right. I'll go with my mother to India."

Now, this isn't the *first* time Shane has come out of the coma. It's happened before. Yet this is the first time Shane's level of consciousness seems sustained. The medical team reports Shane's current MRI and EEG readings look promising. However, Shane's mental status is somewhat confused. Whether it is organic brain damage, amnesia, or some other etiology remains unclear at this point.

Since arriving in India, Ned has called me a few times. He has left several messages. He's excited about his sister's impending birth. I think Ned gets swept up with all the excitement, he forgets about the time zone differences. India is twelve and a half hours ahead of British Columbia. We are quite out of sync.

Tonight, I thought about calling Ned to give an update on Shane's condition, but I went to bed instead. I was too tired to call. Too tired for talking tonight. Of course, wouldn't you know it, one in the morning British Columbia time Ned starts phoning me. I had my cell phone ringer turned off, so his call went direct to voicemail. I needed to sleep. Things have been stressful, sleep helps. If I don't get enough sleep things start to unravel.

We live in my old childhood home in Vancouver's Kitsilano neighbourhood. When our parents died there was some thought about selling the old place. It needed work. Dad wasn't handy. Anyhow, long story made short, Shane and I didn't sell the house. We kept the place up and running. A couple years ago Shane got into some legal trouble. He had participated in a brawl and busted up the Arbutus Street Pub.

Ned's mother worked out a plea bargain deal where Shane was placed on a "Peace Bond." One of the conditions was that Shane should live with his sister's *supervision.* Previously, Shane had been living, for free, in Logan Meyer's basement. It was nothing but trouble in those days. Boys being dumb.

Many modern people have ditched their landlines in favour of new cell phone tech. For sentimental, mostly mental, reasons I never bothered cancelling our landline. I liked the number. It reminded me of our parents. It doesn't ring that often. When it does ring it's usually a politician, telemarketer, or some old family friend who doesn't know our cell numbers. Tonight, however, the stupid thing kept ringing and ringing. I finally couldn't cope, got out of bed, and answered it. Ned was on the other end. He's talking a mile a minute. From what I could gather, Amelia gave birth to a healthy boy. His name is David.

"*I'm an uncle!"* Ned said with glee.

"That's great Ned," I said groggily. "How's Amelia doing?"

"Fine, she's doing just fine. They'll all be coming home tomorrow, or the next day. According to the hospital's rules, only Raj was allowed in the hospital delivery room."

"That makes sense."

"Oh yeah, hospital policy stuff, and we were agreeably obedient."

"Great, thanks for calling Ned. Send some photos, okay. I've got to go back to bed. I'm tired. Good night, love you." I was trying to disconnect.

"Wait, wait," Ned wouldn't let me go just yet, "how's Shane. Anything new?"

Oh well, of course, I had to bring Ned up to speed now. Otherwise, I would feel guilty holding back on him. I knew this would take more time than I'd rather. Sleeping is postponed. I let out a sigh, "Shane's regained consciousness," I replied. "He's alert for short periods of time, but incoherent for much of the time he's awake."

"Yes," Ned replied, "that's what we heard."

"Oh, that's good," I was happy to hear someone in our circle was keeping in touch with the India crowd. "Did Logan call you?"

"No," Ned's tone sounded peculiar.

"Okay," I was curious, "who then."

"Well, I'm probably under the cone of silence credo, but since you are family, I can likely slide you inside."

"Ned," I exhaled, "its late here, I'm tired, *code of silence,* what are you on about?"

"*Cone,* not code," he answered. "It's the cone of silence credo."

"Whatever."

Too often Ned does this weird whistling sound thing through his teeth when he is nervous, "Well, you see, I'm not sure if it's all completely legal, ethical, or above board, but Raj has hacked the British Columbia medical system's data bases. He has access to all sorts of stuff. He says Amelia started the whole thing when Harpreet was fading."

I groaned, "Ned, Harpreet is dead. He didn't fade, he died."

"Yeah, yes, that's what I'm saying. Raj knew about Harpreet's death before we did."

"How so?" my patience, tolerance, and nonsense levels were depleting rapidly.

Again, Ned did the teeth whistle thing, "So, you see," he began to explain, "whenever a nurse, physician or *anyone* enters something on Shane's chart, we get pinged over here in India."

"We," Ned could tell my fatigue threshold was failing. He's a night owl, I'm not, "who's this *we* you are talking about? *Pinged,* what's a ping?"

"Actually, Raj explains this better," Ned was wavering, "I suspect the computer synonym for ping is probably called notification. I don't know it makes a pinging computer sound."

"You know this makes no sense, right?"

"Which part?"

"How did you know about Shane?"

"Well, long story made short, Amelia still holds some sort of British Columbia medical physician researcher data base security clearance privileges. Raj has their computer servers over here in India setup to receive information. And, basically, that's how we knew about Shane."

"Great, what else do you know?"

"Not much," he placated, "you sound sorta angry, how come?"

"Oh," I sighed loudly, "I'm not angry, tired. I'm *tired* Ned. Lots of stressful stuff going on, computer hackings notwithstanding."

"Okay, yes, gotcha," he whispered, "I'll let you go, talk to you later, tomorrow or something. I love you, Nina."

"Ditto Ned."

Thinking to myself, "Amelia's also a lawyer, if she doesn't know what she's doing, who does, eh?"

"Whatever, this is for another day, I'm going back to bed."

What is Biochemistry?

"Science and art are alike because both make you to think."
~Robert (Bobby) Ernest Gordon Tink (1952 – 2020)

"Good morning Shane," Nurse DD was waking me up, *again.* Cheerfully, she said, "Dr. Jarman and I have been talking about putting you on a traditional circadian rhythm cycle schedule."

Although I didn't *really* know what she was talking about, I trust Nurse DD. She has been nothing but *kind*, and ever so patient with me. Logan says DD comes to the hospital to check on me even when it is her day off. Logan says you can't buy that type of devotion. Nina says Logan knows a lot about buying things. He's a pro. Me, I know nothing about nothing. Yet, they all say I'm getting better.

Groggily, I asked, "What kind of schedule have I been on?"

She smiled, sympathetically. I do like her gap-toothed smile. "That's the problem," she explained, "you haven't been on *any* schedule."

"I haven't?"

"Nope," she was messing with my machinery beside the bed, "and you know what they say?"

"No, what do they say?" I asked.

DD gave me the waving pointed index finger, "People don't plan to fail. They fail to make plans. So, we're making plans for you to be normal."

"Normal?"

"Yes, *normal.*"

"Okay, fake it until you make it."

"That's right."

Really what she wanted was for me to get up in the morning. Do things during the day and sleep at night. She says Logan must abide by normal hours, too. No more all-night goofing around parties and pizza.

Logan is what they call an impatient person. My sister, Nina, says he's high-strung, but Logan loves me. They say we are old friends.

Nurse DD has taught me how to use the fancy phone Logan gave me. But she encourages that I should try to not call people in the middle of the night, or at dinner time. Otherwise, the phone is a good thing. People definitely do like it when I call them. All I have to do is say their name or click on their picture and the call goes out. It's been fun to do the FaceTime thing. DD explained that Logan's people programmed the phone for me.

"Logan has people?"

"Yes, employees, is the traditional term."

DD has taught me how to use the interweb, *and* a spoon. Logan had brought in more elaborate electronics. Yesterday he brought a raft of sushi. I struggled with the sticks. So, she gave me a spoon. We chuckle about DD teaching me the spoon thing. "Here, let me show you how a spoon works with sushi."

This interweb is something else altogether. Nurse DD showed me how to type in stuff. Logan says just speak into it because that's easier than typing. DD is old school—she types.

I click clacked typing in my sister's name. A bunch of "hits" were produced along with images. "Don't know what I've done with my life, but my sister Nina has been *busy.*"

"Yes, your sister has worked hard and done well," Nurse DD agreed, "but you have done just fine Shane. You are going to be okay."

"How's that?"

"You stood up to racists before it was fashionable," DD said with emphasis.

"Fashionable?"

"Yes, I've followed your story from the beginning. It's, of course, unfortunate that those boys died, but they shouldn't have been throwing racist taunts in the first place. That rich kid pulled a knife on you. That's how that part started. I've seen the video! It was on the news, repeatedly."

Closing my eyes for a moment, I breathed in deeply, and let it out slowly. Bits and pieces of how I got to this place have been re-told to me a few times. Logan showed me the video. My memory has blocked some stuff, or maybe it's memory decay. I don't know much, but I know it's not good or anything.

I pointed to the computer screen, "Looks like Nina has taken some heat for me."

"How's that?"

"See this headline that reads Dr. Nina Bighill's brother convicted of murder. That can't be a good thing for her career."

DD scrolls down the screen, "Have you seen this video clip?"

"No, what is it?"

"Your lawyer, that Annette Reilly is something else altogether, just watch as she rips into the prison guards who smashed your head into the concrete. She's gonna sue the shirts off those guys."

We watched mainstream traditional news videos. We scanned headlines. I clicked on Nina's bio file and it said, "Dr. Nina Marie Bighill earned a PhD in bio-chemistry at the University of British Columbia. Currently, Dr. Bighill serves as the principal researcher at Pacific Apex Laboratories." I wondered how many labs existed. I wondered how many Nina oversaw.

I wondered, what is *biochemistry?*

I wondered what I should do with the rest of my life.

Glad some life is left to live. Glad I didn't die in the prison.

Mrs. Reilly is a tough lawyer.

Glad she's my lawyer.

Taj Mahal and the Mughals

"Four walls and a roof, that's a building. Architecture is something else altogether."
~The Honourable David Ian Smyth (1947 – 2010)

We were walking towards the Taj Mahal entry lineup. Parm explains, "So, you know, Uncle R, you can't just walk inside. They have security."

Nowadays, I don't *mind* lineups so much anymore. Parm says it's your *mind* to make up. "Don't waste neurons on little things."

At the entrance there is a men's line, and a women's line. I would prefer we stick together, but I can cope being apart momentarily. Parm is most helpful. Don't know what I'd do without her. She speaks the language, explains the situations, and grabs me by the hand when I am to follow with no discussion.

"I don't want you to get run over because your Canadian traffic instincts are backwards over here."

While waiting, the delightful new mobile phone Raj gave me was in my pocket pinging, ringing, and vibrating. I paid it no mind as after four ring cycles it goes to voicemail with a message screen readout. Besides, I've learned its bad manners to take the phone out in a lineup. Respectfulness is easy enough. I can do that. Good manners get you places.

Parm was patiently waiting for me on the other side of the security checkpoint. The women's line is often shorter because more men move about, women not so much. It's India.

"See, that didn't take too long."

"No, that's nothing," I grinned, "where do we start?"

Parm has been here before, so she knows the ropes. On the journey to get here she explained that the ivory white marble Taj mausoleum that sits on the southern bank of the Yamuna River was built close to *four hundred* years ago. The Mughal emperor Shah Jahan commissioned the construction to house the tomb of Mumtaz Mahal. "She was his favourite wife."

"Oh, so this is a love story."

"That's what John Lennon said."

"No, John Lennon said, all you need is love."

"Whatever, you're the expert."

We put on protective booties over our shoes because those were the rules. We walked all around the Taj. The place was a marvelous piece of architecture. We enjoyed every angle, piece of marble, stone and the lighting was fabulous.

"So, is this one of the *seven wonders of the world?"*

"Don't know, but sometimes that stuff is just nothing but buckwos anyways."

"Buckwos?"

"Yeah, you know corporate commercializations of culture."

"True that," I grinned with great contentment. "I hear you sister."

Buckwos is a synonym to bulltweed.

Just then my cell phone device pinged and vibrated to remind me that I have some *ignored* messages waiting. I pulled it out of my pocket. In descending order, I saw three calls from my sister, two from Ned, and one from Raj. Emails are always another story.

"Say Parm," tapping her shoulder, "think you should see my message screen shots."

Message number one from my sister Annette read: Ned and I are coming to India. We want to be there when my grandchild is born.

All the other messages were about their trip logistics, flight numbers, and details.

Ned's message said, "Uncle R, get ready we're coming to get you!"

Raj's message confirmed that they knew the Vancouver Reillys were coming. Amelia was copacetic with everything. She's über pregnant. Raj's parents, still in India, are arriving in Chandigarh soon. "Everyone's going to be here. You and Parmy should get back soon." Then he added, "Tell Parmy to turn her phone on. She's such a cheapskate." Raj ended the message with a chortling noise.

We both laughed.

"What's the difference between a cheapskate and a skinflint?"

"Ask a tightwad."

"That's not funny."

"I know."

I Have *Two* Shrinks

The great Irish-Canadian geotechnical scholar (and sailor), Dr. Peter Byrne (1936 – 2017) said, "Engineering science is putting things together. Figuring out people, that's harder."

"Listen Logan, people have grown tired of hearing you say, sorry."

Currently I have *two* shrinks.

These days, every Wednesday at three in the afternoon, I visit Dr. Walter Conley. Well, almost every Wednesday, sometimes I skip out when things are going on and I have to go with the flow. However, I always try to call his office when that happens.

"Sorry, see you next week." And, of course, I always pay extra fees for standing him up. Delinquent daze and daytime drinking do it to me. I'm trying to be better, but old habits die hard.

Dr. Wally and I talk about my various problems. Over the years, since I was a kid, I've seen a lot of shrinks. Shane and I used to go and see Dr. Shelley together. She was great. Shane and I had been diagnosed with Adolescent Post Traumatic Stress Disorder after we found Banny hanging from a tree. Dr. Shelley preferred *talking therapy* to our taking pills for the PTSD. We were teenagers.

Shane started smoking weed and drinking younger than what would be reasonable. Things started going downhill. It was hard watching the train going off the tracks. Nothing good comes from drinking and smoking too much.

Additionally, every Saturday morning at 9:00 my wife, Wendy, and I go to see Dr. Karen Kranzon for couples counselling. Without fail, every Saturday we are out of bed at eight, getting ready to go and get downtown in time for nine. This is harder for me than Wendy. And that is despite her Monday to Friday time spent attending law school.

"This is a *priority*, Logan." Wendy emphasized with her stern voice.

I know a lot about counselling. Now that doesn't translate into success necessarily, but I do know a lot about counselling. Success, on the other hand, is another story.

When we were twenty-one, Shane had to go to *court ordered* counselling for brawling and behaving badly at the Arbutus Street Pub. He had some anger management problems. The court measured success by the counsellor's report and whether or not Shane got into more trouble. Of course, ever since we were kids, Shane has always been getting into trouble.

Currently, I'm going to *spousal ordered* counselling. Wendy said, "If you go for counselling, I will continue to live with you. If not, I am out of here." I'm not a complete idiot, every Saturday we go to couples counselling with Dr. Kranzon.

Couples counselling is good. Although I am not allowed to monopolize the conversation, my concerns are heard. I'm not allowed to say my current behaviours are due to my parents fighting and subsequent divorce either.

"Logan, we are working for the future. The past is behind you."

"So, you know how some couples hire a babysitter and pay money for childminding. It's the opposite for me. On Saturdays when we go for counselling my dad pays us money to sit with his granddaughter, Banny. It's a win-win situation for everybody."

If our counselling session doesn't end with Wendy being angry with me, we usually go for brunch at the White Spot restaurant on Laurel, and then we visit Shane.

It's been tough times lately. Shane has regained consciousness, which is always good, but he has problems with memory and thinking skills. So, there's the deal with that, you know how it goes with these things. Otherwise, could be worse because he's still here and prison guards didn't kill Shane. They sure messed him up though.

"Bastards!"

What Me Worry

"Crime does not pay as well as politics."
~Alfred E. Neuman (1952 – 2019)

"Good afternoon Nina, this is Susan from the nurse's station calling. Sorry to be calling you at work again, but Nurse Donnelly isn't here, and Dr. Mathison is having some problems with your brother's friend."

"Which one?"

"The curly haired one. I think his name is Mr. Meyers."

"Okay, I'm on my way, I will speak with Logan. Thanks, I will be there shortly." The drive from the UBC lab to the hospital takes fifteen minutes. The car practically drives itself. We've done this route so many times it's like an autopilot function.

I can't fault Logan for being high strung and hot tempered. He has shown such loyalty and dedication to Shane. Some of the physicians won't talk to him, and the ones that do, inevitably get exasperated with him. However, he's deferential to me, and most importantly Logan has Shane's *best* interests at heart.

Logan has spent more time with Shane than anyone. His father is über rich, and Logan receives stipends for sinecure work. Logan has been teaching Shane how to use some of their high-tech equipment. He's got Shane proficiently using a fancy cell-phone and a preprogrammed computer.

Last week, when I stopped by to check on Shane, Logan was there demonstrating with a PowerPoint lesson on how to use their email system. He had a projected series of steps showing how to maneuver email on the wall. Now, every day Shane sends me emails *and* text messages with pictures, audio and video. It's fabulous. This is real progress, Shane is showing advanced thinking, sequencing and seriating skills.

Some of Shane's past long-term memories are returning, but with many large gaps and valleys. Logan placates saying, "No worries Shane, the past is behind us. Let's look forward, we will make new memories!"

Happily, Logan is *also* showing some progressive attitudinal improvements. Their good friend Harpreet Dhaliwal recently died while Shane was in the coma. Logan was devastated by the death. Out of the blue Logan calls and leaves me voicemail saying, "Now that Shane is alert and thinking clearer, I believe it's time to talk to Shane about Harpreet. Would you like to be there with me when this happens?"

I sent him a message saying, "Go ahead, you are the perfect person to talk to Shane about Harpreet. Thanks, but you don't need me for this. Probably best for you two to do this as a duet."

Logan went ahead and spoke to Shane about Harpreet's passing. Shane was nonplussed. He doesn't remember Harpreet, Banny, Ned, Raj, or any of their old gang. He didn't remember me either but has done well working on our relationship. He's curious and asks interesting questions, yet he is confused.

Physically, Shane is showing increasing advances with physiotherapy and mobility. He can walk independently for short distances. He can't climb stairs yet, but they are working on it. All in all, he seems to be getting better.

By the time I arrived at Shane's hospital room Dr. Mathison had left. Shane and Logan were immersed watching YouTube videos about the history of India's partition. They didn't notice me at first, "Hello gents, how's it hanging? Whatcha watching?" I asked.

"Hi Nina," Shane said with a smile, "we're learning about India."

"Okay," I smirked, "what's with that?"

"When the clocks are copacetic, and time zones are cool, we're calling Ned and Raj." Shane seemed so happy.

"You remember Ned and Raj," I asked.

"No, not really, but Logan does."

Logan raised the index finger of doom, "Shane, remember I told you, Ned is our friend." He points to me, "Nina, *your sister,* and Ned, live together in your old family's old house. They aren't married but might as well be. Ned's in India with his mother and Uncle R because his sister, Amelia, is having Raj's baby."

Shane nodded, "Yeah, that's what I said."

"You know you two are both goofballs, right," I said with a scout's salute.

"Logan's worse," Shane salutes in return.

"Really?"

"Ya, you shoulda been here little while ago. Logan got into some shouts with a shrink."

Logan grimaced, "She's not a shrink. She's just a resident."

"Whatever," Shane said holding up two hands in surrender, "they're all the same to me."

"Needles?" Logan spurted.

"Needles are nurses. The docs never give needles. They don't get dirty."

"Surgeons?"

"I'm not having surgery." Shane motioned to me, "Right Nina."

"Yes, that's correct." I agreed.

"See," Shane pointed at Logan.

I didn't want to break the mood, yet thought I should ask, "So what was the problem earlier?"

"Hospital politics," Logan explained curtly.

"How so?"

"Ah, it's nothing really, Karen was making like I was not *immediate* family, and, consequently, I hold no rights to receiving any medical information about Shane."

"Ya, Logan told her to go fuck herself. He's my *brother.*" Shane reported with authority.

"Really."

"Ya, that's what you said. Right, Logan."

He smiled, "Well, something like that."

"How did it end?" I wondered.

"The fuck yourself part, or the other part," Shane pondered.

"What's the other part?"

"Logan's filing an official complaint with the hospital Board of Directors and suing the shit out of her."

"Really."

"Ya."

With a sheepish expression, Logan said, "Well, I was intending on discussing all this with you first."

"No problem Logan, you got it. As far as I'm concerned you *are* Shane's brother! I got your back." I raised my fist in the air.

Shane seemed somewhat confused, "You got his back Nina? What does that mean?"

Logan grinned, "Means we're getting my dad and his lawyers involved. No one pushes us around!"

Shane nodded, "That's great. I like your dad. Gerry's a good guy."

"Yes, he is."

⁂

Later that night, I messaged Logan the old English proverb, "You catch more flies with honey than vinegar."

He replied back within a moment, "Thanks, just politics."

"Okay."

"I'll call you tomorrow. My dad and I are meeting with the VGH's Chief Medical Director, and Board Chair at nine. You are welcome to come if you want. I'll let you know how it goes."

"Okay, thanks."

What could go wrong here? I thought to myself. Still, I knew Logan's dad was a serious special player. If he was there, Logan would be kept in check. Possibly.

Hot heads are hard to predict.

I'm Off Hard Stuff

Delbert Craig Hyde (1950 – 1983) said,
"That's it, I'm off the hard stuff for *good*."

Dad says, "Look Logan, I don't want to appear as an alarmist, but the horizon has some problems looming. I think it's time we bring Shane home."

Of course, that sounded good to me. I didn't even know we could do that, but yes, good idea.

Dad's darkening horizon explanation, however, was certainly concerning. Apparently, there's a respiratory virus quickly spreading in Wuhan, China. Wherever that is. Lots of people are dying at an alarmingly high rate. Dad has a bunch of business contacts, suppliers, and exporters in China. Dad's instincts are kicking in, he knows stuff.

"Listen Logan, likely this virus will hit here sooner or later. This situation might be quite bad."

I liked the idea of springing Shane out of the hospital. "Okay, so have you got doctors lined up to look after Shane?" I asked.

Dad does his typical head movement toss, "Yes, of course, they're working on it. Nurses run the show more than you know. We're currently negotiating with one in particular to see what can be worked out. You know Nurse Diana Donnelly?"

Straight away my spirits lifted, I felt good, "Yeah, yes, she's Shane's favourite nurse."

"Very well then, she's a good nurse, I understand, and the transition should be smoother with her supervision. We will get her to hire, coordinate, and arrange for necessary support staff like physiotherapists, speech therapy, and a shrink or two."

Dad reports that at the best of times a hospital is a good place to get out of because of all the other patients' germs, possible staph infections, and bad air quality. While Shane was comatose the hospital was helpful. Back then it was a good place for him to be. Now it's better to bring him home. This way we have say in rehab programming.

"Dad, did you discuss this with Shane's sister, Nina?"

"No, I prefer you to talk to her, but I am always available, if you need me."

"Thanks."

We Were in the Paramilitary

"When you go one step at a time, it'll add up, and you'll get there, sooner or later."
~Douglas J. McNicol (1955 – 2016)

"So, seriously Shane," Logan asks me with a stern stare, "you really don't remember when we were in the Paramilitary?"

I was sorry to disappoint him, "Nope, I don't. Not at all."

"Well, we were," Logan heaves a heavy sigh, "you, me, Ned, and Raj, we were part of the Kitsilano Cub Scouts Troop. We all would bunk together on cub scout campouts with Ned's Uncle R, as a chaperone. But *he* had to be accompanied by some other *responsible* adult. The head scouts said two adults per cabin were necessary to accompany the boys overnight to prevent perverts from exploiting us."

"Perverts in the Paramilitary?"

"Fuck, yes, perverts in the cub scouts, but not our troop. We'd kick the crap out of them. We were the Kitsilano Crusaders Cub Scout Troop!"

"We would kick their crap?"

"Yes, we would!"

"Okay, whatever you say. You are the leader."

"No, no, Ned is the *Fearless Leader.* While he's gone, I'm only *pro tem.*"

Usually, Logan's a nighthawk, but he was here early at the hospital to tell me, "Shane we've had enough of this place. It's time to take you home."

He said his dad, Gerry, was with hospital administrators doing the paperwork for my release. "Nothing too technical."

"Sure, if you say so." I didn't really understand or know what to think, but my sister, Nina, insists trusting Logan is always a good idea because he holds my *best* interests to heart. "He's a little intense, and high strung, yet he's the best advocate ever," Nina says. "You can trust him."

"Where's my home? With Nina?"

"No way man," Logan laughed. "Nina's working on the Nobel Prize. She's always at her lab. You'd be lonely at her place. You are coming back to your old coach house. It's been renovated. You used to live there before. That is, until one of the courts made an *order* saying you were supposed to live with your sister as a release probation condition or some such legal thing."

"I don't remember, but I'm sure it will be a good thing."

"Did I mention Nurse Diana Donnelly is coming too."

"Nurse DD is going to live with us?"

Logan eye rolled me, "No, silly, she's been hired to coordinate support staff, monitor your progress, and keep the ball rolling."

"Keep the ball rolling. What does that mean?"

I could see he liked the question. "You, my man, Shane Bighill, have been showing very good recovery rehab progress. You are walking. You are talking. And you understand much more now than before."

"I do?"

"Yes, *you do*." Logan smiled, "Ten days ago you didn't know who you were, or what you were doing here."

Thought I should tell him, "You know, for real, I still don't understand very much, right?"

"That's the point!" Logan seemed pleased. "You are doing great. Nurse DD isn't going to actually *live* with us, but she's the boss. DD is in charge. She's going to make sure you *keep* improving. She's got physiotherapists lined up to come to the house. You remember that nice Speech and Language Therapist you liked, Miss Charlotte? She's the one who explains that speech is making the sounds and language is the thoughts. And thoughts are about understanding. Therefore, language is everything."

"Ya."

"Miss Charlotte's on board to do house calls *three* times a week."

Logan seemed so happy with all the plans coming together.

"Okay," although I was confused, I had to ask, "So this has nothing to do with you getting in a squabble with one of the resident doctors yesterday?"

Logan wobbled his head back and forth. "Maybe, you know the straw that breaks the camel's back?"

"Nope, know nothing about camels," I explained.

"Well, when I went home, I explained the incident to my dad. This was *his* idea. He says some shit is sitting on the horizon and it was time to bring you home. At best, hospitals are good to be out of. So, of course, I said, *pitter patter let's get at her!* And here we are. You are going home today."

How long were we in the Paramilitary? Why did we do that?

"Ned and his mum's idea in the beginning. Ned needed structure or some such thing. After that, just peer pressure, we followed suit. We thought the uniforms and badges were cool. Saluting, chanting, and crafting stuff was okay. We especially liked the camping. Cub scouts, Boy Scouts, we had some good times. That's when we were kids."

"When we were kids. What are we now?"

Rolling his eyes, with a sigh, "Not kids."

~

Although things were moving faster than what I was able to completely understand, I thought that this move was a favourable adventure.

In my mind, before falling asleep, or in the middle of the night when I woke, and tried to get back to sleep, I practiced reciting and remembering who's who in our orbit.

Showing Logan, I knew what's what I enumerated, "Ned's sister is Amelia. My sister is Nina. Ned lives with Nina. Raj lives with Amelia. You live with Wendy, Banny, and Gerry. And I'm going home with you to live in the coachhouse."

"That's right," he play-punched my shoulder, "Yes sir, you got it."

"I do, I guess."

"NIKE!"

"Just Do It?"

"With gusto."

"Great."

It's a Fragile Planet

"I'm older than I act, and younger than I look."
~Jesse Winchester (1944 – 2014)

The postpartum period, of course, begins immediately after child-birth. Strange changes. There are the episiotomy medical matters, biochemical changes, hormones, and the various physical aspects. Right now, my body is reacting to my uterus size starting to *try* and return to a non-pregnant level. It's all so topsy turvy.

"OMG, I just pushed out a *baby*."

Social aspects, postpartumly speaking, are another story al-together when compared to the physical condition. Right now, there's a lot of family and folks milling around my house. I think it might be a good thing, but still, it's too soon to know for sure. It's a fluid situation.

My mother and brother, Ned, came for the birthing event. Evidently, my uncle *invited* them, although he insists, he didn't. Raj knew about it but didn't tell me until the last moment. And at the last moment, I cared about nothing.

"Well Amelia, congratulations," my mother said, clapping her hands, "you are a mother now."

"Thanks, I am happy you are here. It's nice you are able to meet your grandson."

"Yes, David's a beautiful boy."

I smiled at her, and said, "Indians say boys are a blessing."

"That's just sexist."

"Thanks mum," I nodded my head, "maybe you might mention that to Raj's people."

"Maybe I will!" She scowled, "but only if someone brings it up first. I promised Ned, nothing but good behaviour here in India."

"Promises, promises." I laughed softly.

During the last couple days my diminished cognitive capacity certainly has been correlated with childbirth conundrums. David is a beautiful boy, but my current reasoning and overall thinking skills are all over the place. My ability to analyze, synthesize, and generate hypotheses hasn't been happening. I've lost my focus. I've caught myself crying for no apparent reason or justified cause. Then I start laughing. I'm *hormonal* and I know it. I don't have postpartum depression. I'm simply hormonal.

My mum's musical hero from the previous century, Joni Mitchell, sang, "laughing and crying, it's the same release." I understand that completely now.

My parents named me Amelia from a Joni Mitchell song. I now know picking a kid's name is not easy. There's a lot of give and take. I understand my father, Thomas, is currently enroute to meet his new grandson. It will be nice to see him. It's been too long.

So, having said that David is a blessing. I must also say a baby girl would have been a blessing, too. Sexism with childbirth makes no sense. We got a boy this go round and that's fine with me. Whether we, meaning *me,* has another baby, well it is just too soon to discuss, but that doesn't stop people from bringing up the topic.

My mother claims having another child is a good idea so that David won't be an *only* child. There was a time when I would have taken the bait and entered her debate. Now I just say, "Yes, thanks, good to know." And I just leave it at that. Blind alley conversations with my mother aren't needed anymore. I've got bigger fish to fry.

On the other hand, my brother, Ned, always laments, "Seriously, I'm so thankful for having a sibling sister. No way I could never deal with mum on my own."

Tilting my head, I can only say, "That's why I'm here."

Since David's birth I haven't been dealing with any electronic messaging, mail, announcements or bulletins. Let the world twirl on without me for a while was what I figured. Today, however, I decided it was time to get back on the electronic wagon. Take a short ride. My mother and David were napping. Raj, Parminder, and Uncle R were on a bicycle excursion for the day. So, I had some rare time to myself.

Like everyone else, these days, I have too many email accounts and messaging systems to manage. I've got the public domain email accounts that receive too many messages, they can wait. I have one *private* email account that only a few have the address. This one has the priority messages that usually need to be read and dealt with first.

Of course, there are always more messages than I would wish from various connections and colleagues. Part way down the list I see *three* from Gerald Myers. I had to think for a second until I realized, "Gerald Meyers, that's Logan's dad."

I knew that he had been the driving force to take Shane out of the hospital and set him up at their place. Logan has hot air to spew but struggles to follow through. His father has more finesse. Gerald Meyers is a somebody who delivers.

At first, I just thought, "Removing Shane from the hospital, rich people are always like that. Stay out of their way." Yet the more I thought about it the more it made sense. It's always better to *not* be in a hospital, unless it's necessary. I was happy to hear Shane's condition was improving. It's been unnerving with him coming out of the coma and then relapsing. Hope this prognosis sticks.

Although I thought my priority email address was private, I also know guys like Gerald Meyers get access to what they want. And I wondered, why's Logan's dad emailing me?

His first email subject line read: *Novel Coronavirus—Wuhan, China.*

Now I earned a medical degree from UBC, but I'm no expert on infectious diseases. Still, I know the novel ones are always lousy. These are the emergent viruses that scientists haven't previously identified and recorded. Unlike chicken pox, measles or other traditional viruses, the novel virus can spread from and animal host to humans. That's never good.

I wondered, why is Gerald Meyers emailing me? What is this COVID-19 he is citing? Why is he noting Wuhan, China? It is the capital city of Hubei province. So, what's the point Gerald? Where are you going with this? Why me? No one told him, "Amelia is a bit busy these days."

Gerald's subsequent emails explain that his *people* have been reporting some strange illnesses originating from Wuhan. This new Coronavirus is spreading extremely fast, people are dying quickly, and in large numbers. Clearly, a *pandemic* has started. We need to talk about this. Please give me a call.

Surprise, surprise, a pandemic, all of this was news to me. I started investigating. I couldn't give Gerald a call right now because of the time zone differences. Besides I thought it would be good to check into his warnings ahead of time before talking over the phone. So, I started to search for data base clues and cues. My British Columbia data base search files were not showing anything. I next moved to European and Asian sources. *Bingo*, some hits came up.

Like our Farmer's Markets in Vancouver, China has these things called Wet Markets where live animals are sold to the public. The animal is slaughtered when purchased. Blood flows freely in these markets. Ethnocentrism notwithstanding, apparently the evidence is suggesting the live animal market in Wuhan is where the novel coronavirus started super spreading. However, the current evidence is not definitive.

Gerald subsequently wrote in the next email that on a macro level this new COVD-19 virus is likely similar to the 1918 pandemic. That was one of the worst pandemics in history. However, Gerald says "This *new* novel virus has the potential to be much *worse!*"

I don't know how this one could be much worse because the 1918 pandemic killed millions of people. Over a hundred years ago, back then, many called that pandemic the *Spanish Flu*. It wasn't true, later historical evidence explained that Spain was likely *not* the place of origin for the virus. But, whatever, that's how those types of things develop.

Spain was neutral and was not involved with WWI. Therefore, their censors started describing the deadly virus with ensuing deaths in real time. The virus concurrently existed in a number other war-torn countries in 1918, but their media censorship did not publish the pandemic. No one knew what was going on due to media censorship. Ouch, they claimed it was for citizens' morale.

I called the number Gerald had sent as his *preferred* telephone number. Of course, I got his voicemail, "Hello Mr. Meyers, this is Amelia Reilly calling. You sent an email asking me to call you. Okay, well, I will call back later, or you can call me. Thanks." I hung up.

Thinking that was a lame message to leave. I'm not feeling very erudite these days. Don't know what I am thinking these days. Now I'm freaked out, thinking about the virus, and what it all means.

I suddenly snapped out of my daydream when I heard David making baby cooing noises and my mother singing, "I've seen clouds from both sides now."

Mr. Meyers is going to be back burnered, for now.

David needs me.

I'm breastfeeding.

Microbes Not Missiles

"The bigger they are the harder they fall. But you know it's always some small thing that takes them down. They always think a big thing will come to get them. It's the small stuff. Just like the thousand paper cut thing."
~The Honourable Anne K. Wallace (1953 – 2015)

"I have felt guilty about Logan for a long time now."

Dr. Talbot raised her eyebrow slightly, "Was that something you wanted to discuss again, Gerry?"

"Oh, I don't know," pursing my lips, "what more I can say."

"Where does your sense of guilt come from?"

Raising my index finger, "You know I was supposed be with Logan and his friends on that Cub Scouts camping trip?"

"What happened?"

"Got in an argument with my ex-wife, Sheila. Stormed out of the house in a huff and bailed on Logan. He went without me."

She shook her pen hand, "No, I meant what happened on the camping trip?"

"Oh, I'm sure I've told you before. The boys stumbled on a suicide pact."

Nodding her head, "I understand, that must have been difficult."

"It was, he was twelve."

"A tender age."

I raised both palms in the air, "You know, he looks like me, he inherited many of my genetic personality traits and foibles, but he's different. He's better than me. Logan is a good man."

"Are you implying that you don't think you are a good man?"

"Not like Logan, I'm afraid." With a smile, and a thumbs up signal, I said, "Logan's a good kid. I'm proud of him."

~

My hour of psychotherapy with Dr. Talbot zinged by too quickly. I got back to my car, checked my messages, saw Amelia Reilly had left me voicemail. Immediately I called her back, only to get her voicemail.

"Hello Amelia, it's Gerry calling, looks like we are doing some telephone tag. Ok, right then, well, you can call me *anytime,* day or night. We've got things to discuss. Thanks."

~

In 2014 Barack Obama explained that microbes were more likely to do damage to the world order rather than missiles.

New Normal is Near

The University of Alberta's Director of the Centre of Experimental Sociology, W. David Pierce (1945 – 2020) said, "Behaviorism and empirical facts are one thing, political discourse is another. It's important to account the differences. And that's what we do."

"Shane, I'm not here to be right, I'm here to get it right."

"Thanks Mr. Meyers, my sister says I should say we appreciate everything you are doing for me."

"Call me Gerry."

"Okay, thanks Gerry."

He sighed, "And Shane, you should know, I'm happy to help anyway I can. I'm here for you. Anything you need, name it, you got it."

"Thanks, I'll start thinking about things I need. I can't think of anything right now, but I'll let you know." I didn't know what else to say but that seemed to suffice.

I spend some time being confused each day. I don't think that's improving as much as the others, however, Logan says, "Just think of yourself as a *work in progress.*"

Earlier that morning I was still deep sleeping when Logan and his father showed up suddenly at the hospital to get me out. They were moving me into their renovated coach house. Logan says some people call it a *lane-way house* because one of the entrances is in their back alley. The coach house is separate and not attached to the big house. Logan says I've stayed there before, but I don't really remember. Sometimes I will say I remember things just so people feel better about my recovery progress. Sometimes I think I do remember some things, sorta, but most things are fuzzy. Nurse DD says don't let well-meaning folks plant memories.

I feel like I'm definitely a step up from a vegetable garden. So that's my current situation. Nina says, "Don't worry about it."

She's a vegetarian. Hence, vegetables are her thing.

Logan explains I was like a vegetable for a while, but now I'm not.

~

Logan's father talks fast with animation. He waves his arms while he talks.

"Shane, you see this button?" Seems both Logan and his Pops are big on the buttons business.

"Yes," I nodded.

"Push it whenever you want *anything*. It will softly set off a buzz in the big house and a blue light will blink in the kitchen. Another blue light will blink in Logan's room, too. Logan insists blue is the colour you two share. So, blue it is. And if I can do anything, just push the yellow button on your phone, tablet, or laptop. I'll come running."

"Okay."

~

That day as soon as we got to the coach house Logan said he had to vamoose, discuss things with Wendy, and look after his daughter, Banny, because Wendy had to do something somewhere.

Their counsellor says Logan should be more accommodating to Wendy's requests. He says he's trying. Wendy says, "Try harder."

Logan gave me a firm hug, he got a little weepsy, and said, "I gotta go. I can hear my Pops coming. He's gonna show you around the place. Don't worry, he's cool, and he's happy you are here. Things are gonna be alright Shane. You'll see."

And with that there was a rap, tap, tap on the door, Logan's Pops came rolling in. He grabbed my shoulders, smiled, and said, "We are all awfully happy you are here, Shane. Hope you are going to be comfortable living here. Nurse DD is scheduled to see you tomorrow morning."

That made me smile. "Thanks, she's helpful."

Nina says stuff is going on in the world right now. "Logan's people have an inside track on the situation, and that's a good thing. People don't want you to worry needlessly."

"Okay."

What do I know anyways? This morning I was in the hospital, now I'm not. Before that I was in some prison in Saskatchewan for something I did, but I don't remember doing it. The prison guards smashed my head on the concrete floor for something I did or didn't do to them. After that, I went into a coma. Ned's mother is my lawyer, she got me outa Saskatchewan.

All things considered, looking around my new home I'd have to say, "This is good. This is a better place to be."

Logan keeps saying, "These days, this is the *new normal.*"

Okay, new normal, fine by me because I can't remember the old normal. So, whatever, new normal doesn't matter much to me.

Nurse DD says, "Don't sweat the small stuff. And remember, most stuff is small stuff."

She explains that we must work on improving my information processing skills. And more importantly, *we* need to work on my comprehension, "Reading between the lines is just as important as reading the lines.

"I can read."

They all seem to say they think I'm getting better. I don't know about that, yet it's good to be out of the hospital. Got my own fridge here. DD explained refrigerator principles to me. It's quite cool how they did that, eh? DD says her grandfather had an *icebox*. Fridges hadn't been invented back then.

DD disclosed that in addition to her nursing training, she holds physiotherapist credentials. Consequently, that's why we started doing *walking therapy* as soon I got on my feet with a certain level of stability. "Falling is bad. You don't want to fall at all. With a fall, consequences can be dire."

"Okay, I'm not going to fall, not on purpose, of course." Pratfalls were what we did in middle school. I remember that. Someone got hurt, but I can't remember who. Logan says he purposely forgets shit.

DD went on to explain the *no pain no gain* mantra some people speak about is complete and utter nonsense. "Pain has *meaning*. If your brain is sending you messages indicating a pain signal, then that means something is not right. Pushing through the pain could cause damage. We want recovery progress. Damage doesn't cut it with our program."

"We have a program?" I asked.

"Yes," she nodded, "that's why I'm here. You betcha, we got a programme planned, drawn out and ready to go."

We walked and talked every day. It was good, I liked it. I always looked forward to our walkabouts. DD explained things to me in a way I could understand and then repeat back to my sister, Nina. It was a validity check. If I could understand and explain to Nina, that was a good thing.

DD explained cancer to me. I didn't have the understanding or frame of reference she had. Previously, DD worked as a nurse in the cancer ward for a long time. "Too long," she says.

Nina was impressed when I re-framed the heterogeneous aspects of cancer cells to her while we ate homemade pizza. "Remember our Uncle Harry," I asked, "he died from lung cancer, right?"

"Yes," she nodded, reaching to pour some ale.

I was starting to roll it out, "Smoking cigarettes causes cancer, right. Everyone agrees on that."

"Yes, for the most part, they do."

"Alright, but as DD describes, there are additional contributing factors to make an accurate accounting."

Nina raises her eyebrow, "Okay."

"So, smokers likely drink more alcohol and coffee, compared to nonsmokers. At work, during coffee break, the smoker doesn't eat an apple, but smokes instead. Therefore, their diet becomes a contributing factor."

"Makes sense."

"And then there is their personality that kicks in as a factor."

"How so?"

"These days, *anyone* who smokes does so in the face of all scientific medical evidence. The tide turned on smokers. So, their defiant personalities contribute."

Nina smiled, she seemed happy to hear me rattle on about stuff she knows about because she's a biochemist, but the idea that I was engaged and explaining things made her happy. "Makes sense to me." She popped the top of another ale.

"Logan said he thought some people get cancer because of bad luck or something like a health accident. Sorta like what happened to our parents?"

Nina took a deep sigh, "Well, yes, I guess," she looked at me with a forlorn gaze, "that's one way of looking at life."

I was trying to read *between* her lines like DD suggested, "What were our parents like? I don't remember much about them."

"They were great parents, Shane." She smiled, "I'll bring you some pictures."

"Thanks."

Nina cleaned up our dishes, kissed me on the forehead, smiled, and said, "I have to go now, lab work waiting, be back tomorrow. Call me if you need me. Okay?"

"Yes, okay, for sure, I kissed her on her forehead, "See you tomorrow. Are you cool to drive after two beers? Logan says these days, if you have had a beer or know someone who had a beer, you will get busted for drinks and driving. And that's become a bad behaviour thing."

Nina smiled, "I'm impressed with the *new* Logan! That's real progress for sure. He used to be such an asshole." She added, "And for the record, I had a beer and a half, which is well within the parts per thousand blood alcohol legal limits. See you tomorrow Shane."

"Yes, thanks."

I didn't know that side of Logan.

Did I?

Kelsey – Puerto Rico

Ilka Chase (1905 – 1978) said,
"The only people who fail are those who don't try."

"Hey, K, did you know Puerto Rico translates from Spanish meaning Rich Port," Edilma enthusiastically explained as we were planning my sojourn south. "You will love this little island nestled in the archipelago among the Greater Antilles. It's an awesome place to be. This is my happy place."

Vancouver gets a lot of rain in the winter. Going to Puerto Rico, the *Rich Port,* to work on Edilma's project seemed like a fabulous idea. "I've never been anywhere exotic."

On one hand Edilma told me to pack for warm weather, on the other, "Don't pack too much stuff. No bling or anything someone would want to steal. And some sensible shoes, you'll need those."

Edilma is always big on *sensible shoes.* To the contrary, Caitlyn always wears expensive crazy shoes. I'm somewhere in between. Still, I'm bringing some favourite flip flop footwear. Whatever, that's the deal. I like flip flops in warm weather. I don't want sweaty feet. I rotate between three colours—green, blue, and red. Although I think I will probably bring black ones, too.

Martin, my neighbour from down the hall, lent me his fancy carbon fibre framed grey backpack with a Canadian flag patch sewn on the back, "This pack took me across Africa, and back," he explained. "sturdy, but light weight, and can carry lots of stuff. Kelsey, you'll be in good shape with this lucky pack. Besides, it has good traveling karma."

Now that made me feel confident—*traveling karma*. That's sweet.

~

Departure day seemed like the clock's numbers sped by faster than I anticipated, but all things considered, everything went well. Martin drove me to the Vancouver Airport. Traffic was light, I passed through security easily, and I got a window seat. The first flight was direct from Vancouver to Miami. The next connecting flight was from Miami to San Juan, Puerto Rico.

Final goodbye airport hugs, "Just two jaunts," I told Martin, "and then I'll be there."

"Yes, just two jaunts," he gave me a hard hug, "send back a message so I know you got there safely."

With that my watery eyes and I took off for the trip.

~

The Miami airport was awfully big, bustling with lots of noise. I was happy that the flight was on time. I checked the big screen in the hallway. Connecting flights always make me nervous. Actually, airports make me nervous. Martin's backpack was checked straight through. It was out of my hands and destined for San Juan. *All* I had to do was make sure I got to the correct gate on time to catch the connecting flight.

Of course, I can't identify airplanes by their design numbers or manufacturers, but I do know this one flying from Miami to San Juan was smaller, bumpier, and I had to quell some nervousness until safely landing. I sympathize with people who have a fear of flying, especially over the ocean. Turbulence terrifies me.

Fortunately, we finally landed safely. I didn't get sick. Next task was luggage recovery. I went to the confusing baggage area zone. Glory be, my bag was waiting, on the conveyor belt. I pulled the backpack on and made my way to the exit. I was expecting to see Edilma somewhere in the crowd. Scanning from side to side there was no sign of Edilma.

Outside the baggage area there were lots of people milling about with signs and stuff. It was noisy. A small amount of anxiety was creeping in on me and then I saw a tall woman with a sign saying: KELSEY PEARCE.

She spotted me, started waving the sign. Muscling her way through the crowd she approached sticking out her hand to shake, "Hi Kelsey, I'm Sojo," she smiled. "I recognized you from the phone photos Edilma had shown me. You looked great in the photos, but better in person!"

"Thanks, I guess, where's Edilma?" I asked.

"She is back in town meeting with some heavy hitters who are financing part of the project. She couldn't leave them hanging. So, she sent me. Nice to meet you, Kelsey. Edilma is excited you are coming to work with us. She says you are a *fabulous* friend."

"Thanks," At that point, I felt happy to have safely arrived, I am not too nervous about flying and traveling in general. However, all this mayhem made me slightly nervous, "nice to meet you Sojo. I appreciate you picking me up."

"My pleasure."

I thought her name, Sojo, was a derivation from the French word sojourn—to take a trip. But, no way, it wasn't, her parents, Trevor and Anne Roberts, named their only child after the American abolitionist, Isabella Baumfree (1797 – 1883), aka Sojourner.

In 1843, after Isabella had become convinced that God had called her to be an activist, Isabella gave herself the name *Sojourner Truth.* She had become a powerful orator who gave many important speeches.

Sojourner Truth was a great American abolitionist. A strong singer, too. When she died, the magnificent Frederick Douglass gave her eulogy. It was a large service, many people were there to pay respects, and honour Sojourner Truth's work. It was 1883 and the world was ever so slowly turning towards something.

My new fast friend, Sojourner Roberts, and I connected almost immediately. She is so cool! Edilma must have paranormally sensed the connection. I'm so glad she sent Sojo to meet me at the San Juan airport.

I asked Sojo Roberts how she ended up here in Puerto Rico. Sojo explained that after she had finished writing her master's thesis about the poet, scholar, and writer, George Santayana (1863 – 1952), she needed something to do for a *gap* year. She had already been accepted into the medical school in Edmonton, but she had also been offered a scholarship to attend the PhD programme in creative writing at the University of Calgary. She needed some time to decide which direction to travel.

That was back in September 2017, after hurricane Maria had hit Puerto Rico hard, killing close to *three thousand people.* Sojo hasn't left yet.

"I love it here," Sojo explained, "maybe it's the Puerto Rican people or the food like arroz con gandules, who knows, I haven't been able to get it together to go back home. I'm not ready, yet. My mum is a physician, she's not happy, but hey, I'm twenty-six years old. I decide what's best for me. Originally, I was going to stay for a year to help with hurricane relief work."

"What happened?" I asked. "Why have you stayed so long?"

"There's still lots of work that needs to get done."

I remember the time when Edilma, Parminder, Caitlyn and I went to a big party at Ned Reilly's house. He was wearing a bright red T-shirt that said: *Don't Ask About my Thesis.*

Parm's brother, Raj, is Ned's best friend, he said, "Go ahead ask him."

We didn't. Rather Caitlyn and I went to the bar in the back where Logan was the bartender passing out drinks, provided you answered his *skill testing question.*

Caitlyn said, "Fuck you Logan, that's the password, give me two of the coldest beer you got back there."

He complied and passed Caitlyn two cold beers.

Caitlyn winked at me, "That's how you do it."

"Thanks," we clinked our bottles together, "cheers."

Although I didn't dare ask, who was I anyway, nothing but an interloper at the party. Still, I wondered about Ned Reilly's T-shirt. What was the meaning behind it? Was it latent or blatant? A play on words with esoteric meaning. Did he *want* to talk about his thesis? Or was it a sarcastic shirt? You know, at this point he's satiated, fed up and doesn't want to talk about the thesis. Just leave me alone type of thing, maybe.

Sojo said after she finished writing her thesis, she needed something to do during a *gap year.* She ended up in Puerto Rico. Three years after thesis completion, here she was picking me up at the airport in an old beat-up truck.

"Nice truck," I said with a slight snarky overtone, "it'll get us to where we want to go, right?"

Sojo simply smiled, "Yep, there and back, again."

"Good to know," I nodded with an appreciative understanding.

Turns out there have been a bunch of car jackings in Puerto Rico recently. "If you are driving an old beat-up truck the chances of getting jacked are less. But we take nothing for granted on these roads."

Sojo seemed so confident. Of course, I noticed a firearm quietly jutting out from under her seat.

"So Sojo, what made decide to write a thesis about George Santayana?" I asked. "I've never heard of him."

"Sure, you have," she smiled, "you just need some context. Santayana was the man who wrote *Those who cannot remember the past are doomed to repeat it.*"

"Okay, yes, I've heard *that* aphorism," I said with a nodding smile.

"George Santayana is also famous for writing: "*Only the dead have seen the end of war.*"

"Oh, that's a good one. I haven't heard that before." I started singing, "War, what is it good for?" With a big grin I explained "Eric Burdon sang that one."

Sojo smirked, she started singing, "I've looked at clouds from both sides now, from up and down, and still somehow, it's clouds illusions I recall, I don't know clouds at all."

Oh, I know that one. My dad sings that song, "That's Joni Mitchell from Saskatchewan!" I replied with some zest.

Sojo said, "Yes, the one and only Joni." We both started singing while we were driving down the road winding our way to the project site.

Over the next few weeks Sojo taught me many things while we worked together on Edilma's project. Certainly, I was quickly becoming a quasi-Santayana scholar. Sojo loved talking about him. I learned that he anglicized his name from Jorge to George while attending Harvard where he earned a PhD. Santayana worked hard studying under the guidance of the famed psychologist and philosopher, William James. In addition to scholarly work, Santayana was a writer and a cartoonist for the infamous Harvard Lampoon. "That's cool!"

From 1889 to 1912 George Santayana worked as a professor at Harvard. He had many notable students who became famous in their own right. T.S. Eliot, Walter Lippman, W.E.B Du Bois, and Wallace Stevens were some of Santayana's students and long-time friends.

In 1912 Santayana resigned from Harvard. He had received an inheritance and had saved enough money be free from academia. Sojo said, "He didn't hate working at Harvard, yet the opportunity to leave academic obligations behind was attractive. He could do as he pleased without academic responsibilities and the accompanying duties."

George Santayana spent the next forty years in Europe until his death in Rome, September 26, 1952. He was a preeminent scholar, philosopher and a poet. A productive eighty-eight years of writing, teaching and cultivating colleagues.

Sojo sent me an emailed copy of her thesis. Three hundred, forty-five pages. That'll be a reading.

It was a sunny Saturday afternoon, February 14, 2020, also known in some commercialized circles as Saint Valentine's Day.

Sojo and I had driven the old green-latrine beat-up truck to the southern coastal city of Ponce to pick up plantains, oranges, and electrical equipment. We had a lovely lunch at a restaurant that was advertised as "José Feliciano used to live here."

After lunch we went to the produce place. We got almost everything on the list. Sojo is so good at haggling. I'm not. "No, no, no," shaking her head, waving her hands in the air, "that's too much money, my boss will be mad at me if I waste money. No can do at that price."

Then they settle. They always settle, but negotiations are the prelude. It's a dance. I'm clumsy, don't like the dance steps, but happy to serve as Sojo's haggling foil. It's part of her skill set. Not mine, however, I hate haggling.

When we finally returned to the project site, started unloading, Edilma came strutting down the driveway to the parking place, "We have to talk." She gave the arm up follow me signal.

"Sure," Sojo said, "first we'll unload this stuff and be available straight away."

Edilma shook her head, "No, come inside now. We have to talk, stuffs happening, and we got to get things sorted out."

I dropped the heavy cardboard box back in the truck, looked over at Sojo with raised eyebrows. She shrugged, and we followed Edilma. Sojo whispered to me, "Stuffs happening?"

Sojo and I looked at each other quizzically, shoulder shrugs, jumped out of the back of the truck, and followed along behind Edilma. Unlike Sojo, I've known Edilma since forever. So, if she says something is serious, it is. I could tell this is going to be big. I thought to myself, "Likely nothing good is happening here."

The project's conference room and dining room were both one and the same. Some of the other project workers, as well as volunteers had been gathered. Nydia, Luis, James, and Susie were sitting around the table. Of course, everyone had a laptop open or was fiddling around with their phone. "Kay passé," I asked cheerfully. "What's happening at this little happy get together?"

Susie threw us a shoulder shrug and said, "We've been waiting for you two to arrive. Kevin and Ronnie are in the kitchen cooking. They will drop respective spatulas and come running to this meeting when Edilma calls it open."

"Okay," I winked, clicked my tongue, sat down, and said, "that's cool. What are they cooking?"

"Who knows," Luis replied with a grin, "smells good though."

A moment or two passed when Edilma came shuffling in, sat down at the head of the table, and said, "Ronnie's still on the phone." She smiled, "we'll give them a minute, and then get started."

Kevin came flying in with his usual flair, landed at the table with a bit of commotion, and mouthed, "He's coming."

Ronnie strolled in, sat down, and asked, "Where's the fire? Unlike you all, I've got work waiting." He always rolls his eyes.

Edilma let out a sigh, pursed her lips, and began to explain what has happened and what was going to happen. She had been on the telephone with our friend Parminder Gill for an hour this morning. Parm is currently in the Punjab with family and friends. "We are shutting the project down for a while," Edilma said with a sad tone. "Kelsey and Sojo," she looked at us, "we're making arrangements to fly you back to Canada, immediately."

Sojo groaned, "Sounds stupid," with an open palm slap on the table, she asked, "What's going on?"

Edilma closed her eyes for a moment, "First, let me finish what I have to say before we start discussing things that are already fait accompli."

Sheepishly, Sojo slowly raised her hands in the air flashing peace signs and silently mouthing, "Sorry." In her mind, however, she was saying, "I'm not ready to go home. We've still got work to do here."

Edilma was getting a bit more flustered. Nevertheless, she was determined to get everyone to understand what was happening, the gravity of it all, and why the urgency to get ahead of the curve was important. "So, I spent close to an hour this morning talking to Parminder and her sister-in-law, Amelia. They are in India tracking and monitoring the developing pandemic."

Kevin can't keep quiet at these things. He made a whistling sound, and said, "Pandemic, sounds bad, ouch."

Nodding her head in agreement, Edilma said, "Yes that's correct Kevin." Then she exhaled heavily, "So, here's the deal as it's been explained to me. Three days ago, the WHO."

Kevin interrupted because he can't keep quiet and slow down his piffling. "Who's the WHO?"

Patiently, yet with a level of consternation, Edilma replied, "The World Health Organization, a specialized agency from the United Nations, has declared that a virus is fast becoming a major international problem."

Unobtrusively, Ronnie kicked Kevin under the table, lifted an eyebrow so as to communicate—cool it and quiet down.

"On February 11," Edilma continued, "this new virus strain was named as COVID-19. CO, representing *corona,* Vi indicates *virus,* D means *disease,* and 19 portrays the year 2019 identified." Raising her index finger for emphasis, "This is only the sixth time in history where the WHO has declared a global emergency."

Luis raised his hand and asked, "What does that mean?"

"It means a lot of people are going to die," Ronnie answered.

"Okay, no way I can see Puerto Rico hospitals able to handle the upcoming surge," Sojo suggested. "The San Juan hospital struggles at the best of times."

And that was that. A small amount of chit chats and woe is me chants followed and then we went our separate ways.

I sort of knew Logan Meyers from previous parties in Vancouver, but I didn't know too much about him other that his father is wealthy. Logan is friends with my friend Parminder's brother. Turns out they are all on top of things much more than we are in PR.

Logan arranged for an airplane to divert from Haiti to come and pick me up at the San Juan airport. All I had to do was be there at the correct time. Edilma pleaded, made a case to squeeze Sojo onto the same plane. We would travel together to Vancouver. Then Sojo was supposed to go back to Calgary. That's the plan.

Edilma explained she was not coming with us. She planned to ride out this pandemic here in PR. She's got some family on the other side of the island. She can't leave them behind. "They're family."

The next day we went to the San Juan airport. With too many tears to shed we took off vowing that: "We will return!"

GENOGRAMS

"The illiterates of the 21st century will not be those who cannot read and write, but those who cannot learn, unlearn, and relearn."
~Alvin Toffler (1928 - 2016)

"These days young psychologists have it easy," I explained to Parminder while we waited for the Canada Border and Customs Officer to give us a clearance sheet. "Prior to computers, we had to do genograms by hand. Nowadays computers do *everything* automatically and easily."

"Genograms," she looked at me with a scowl, "What are you talking about?"

"Seriously, we did genograms with pen and paper. Nowadays young shrinks have it exceptionally easy."

We had just landed back in Vancouver from India on one of the private airplanes owned by the Meyers family corporation. We were waiting on the tarmac for official deplaning clearance forms. My niece, Amelia, had placed all the names in family pods for traveling purposes.

In addition to family pods, Amelia had everything computer charted like a large complex genogram for our departure from India. This new novel coronavirus was descending, or maybe I would be correct to say it was ascending faster than expected. Either way Amelia had made arrangements with Gerry Meyers to get us all out of India expeditiously. I don't personally know Mr. Meyers, but I certainly know his son, Logan.

Commercial flights out of India had become difficult to secure. We were fortunate to be connected to Mr. Meyers. He and Amelia are more than panicked about the spread of COVID-19. It's not that some of us were nonchalant or anything, yet the gravity of everything was fast overwhelming. Understanding this was all new.

Way back when I was a young psychologist, emboldened with a freshly printed licence to practice, I thought I knew all that was needed to be known about diagnosing a number of mental conditions.

People walking down the street talking to themselves, cursing and shouting always made me think schizophrenia. Nowadays with mobile phone's earpieces and microphones it seems lots of mostly normal people trundle down the street talking to themselves.

Bobby Dylan's song was prophetic: the times they are a-changing.

Autism, schizophrenia's cousin, was one of those things I thought, as a young shrink, I knew what was what about the diagnostic condition. When I worked at the hospital, we had a number of autistic patients. I felt confident we were helping to understand their condition. Now I wonder. Now I'm a lot humbler about the things I might not hold all the diagnostic answers. It's not that easy anymore. A label or pigeonhole is bad, but identification for treatment seems helpful.

"Refrigerator mums," grimacing, I recalled when I first started studying autism, the science of the day said etiology was a direct correlation between something that the mother did or didn't do that caused the child's autism. "Nowadays everyone knows it's neurological. There's no debate."

Psychology evolves, I explained to Parm, "Imbecile, moron, idiot, and retard were all once good, clean, diagnostic terms used to classify people. These days, those terms are despicable. No one uses them professionally, popular parlance, that's a different matter."

Bruno Bettelheim, from the University of Chicago wrote a book about autism in 1967. He compared autism to being a prisoner in a concentration camp. Bettelheim was an expert. People believed him. And it took too much time to turn that conceptual ship around in the correct direction.

Parm was getting bored. I could tell my pontificating was not as interesting as I thought. Recently, Parm commented on my sense of humour, "You are the funniest guy you know, right?"

Jokes are relative. Theories are different.

"Wonder how long we will have to wait here?" Parm asked shifting around in her seat looking to see how far the agent had advanced from the back of the plane.

I poked her arm, smiled, and said, "You know what I learned from those long lineups in India?'

Parm rolled her eyes, "What, pray tell?"

"Patience."

Just then the Border and Canadian Customs Officer appeared standing beside our seats, and she asked, "Passports please."

Yodelayheehoo

"Sometimes I go too far. That doesn't mean I am crazy. Just having some fun."
~Hollis Downes (1952 – 1974)

Logan—Whenever I start to think my side of the family is too far gone on the wrong side of nutsy, Lucy, my wife's sister calls and makes me feel better about my people and their abhorrent behaviours…every time without fail. Therefore, I like Lucy, always have. My wife, Wendy, seems skeptical. I don't know why that would be.

I waited a minute or two, until she was off the phone, "So Wendy," I had to ask, "what was your sister singing about today?"

"Well, at first, she said don't tell Logan about this, but at the end of the call she said go ahead because in the long run it really doesn't matter."

"Oh geez, wait, just a sec or so," I went into the kitchen and poured a bag of chips into a bowl. "Okay, I'm ready, spill the beans."

Days turn to weeks and then to months the pandemic restrictions have been rough for most people. Mind you, regular life last year was rough enough for Lucy. Now with the COVID-19 pandemic restrictions, everything gets exacerbated for Wendy's sister, Lucy.

"Some people are like that," was what Wendy always says when we talk about Lucy.

This time was no different than the last, in terms of loony thinking.

Then Wendy did the trumpet blubbering thing with her lips exhaling air with a weird noise. "Lucy says she committed suicide yesterday."

"Yesterday, but you just spoke to her two minutes ago. What's the deal?"

"Lucy met a guy on one of those internet romance dating app sites. They got together yesterday afternoon for an in-person social distance coffee session. One thing led to another, and they ended up going back to his house. Evidently, they had passionate sex all night long. Now she's back home and is convinced she's caught COVID-19 from him."

I didn't want to laugh, but I asked, "Remember the good old days when you lectured Lucy about unprotected sex and birth control?"

Wendy walked away saying, "Ya, I miss the *good old days!*"

Suicide, eh? Well, homicide, the antithesis would be worse.

"I like Lucy!" I yelled as Wendy left the room.

"No, you don't."

"Yes, I do!"

Although Wendy doubts my sincerity, I definitely like Lucy. She's a jewel!

Timing is Everything

John Lennon (1940 – 1980) said,
"Everything will be okay in the end. If it's not okay, it's not the end."

"Shane, you sleeping?"

"Not now I'm not," I answered, "what's going on Logan?"

He let out a sad sigh, sat beside me on my bed, and said, "Lucy got the virus."

"Wendy's sister, Lucy," I asked, "that Lucy?"

"Do you know another Lucy?"

"No, not really, and I don't really know your Lucy neither. She's your sister-in-law, right."

"Yeah, and Wendy is freaking out, big time."

I reassured him, "I'm sure this must be difficult for Wendy. How'd Lucy catch the virus?"

"Contact tracers are trying to figure out how she got exposed, and who Lucy might have subsequently exposed. She called Wendy tonight to say she's in the UBC hospital, but due to COVID, *no visitors allowed.*"

I thought to myself, and then said out loud, "I can't remember when I last saw Lucy. Must have been at your party. How about you? When did you see her last?"

Logan makes this weird whistling noise with his lips when he is stressed out. "Dunno," he murmured, "Wendy talks to Lucy over the phone *all the time*. Lucy's not in our direct family pod bubble for visitors. We haven't been face to face with Lucy in months. Wendy does video and audio *chats*."

"Maybe Lucy got it where she works?" I wondered out loud.

"No," Logan chortled, "Lucy has been working from home since the pandemic started."

"What does Lucy do from home?"

"Dunno, she's an accountant," Logan snorted.

"She's an accountant. What do they do from home?" I asked naively.

"Count stuff, I guess." Logan exhaled heavily, "I'll see you later. I gotta get back to the big house in case I'm needed."

"Okay," I didn't really know what else to say, "good idea, see you later."

And just as fast as Logan had breezed in, he was gone.

I rolled over and went back to sleep.

Three days later, Lucy was put on a ventilator. I messaged Nina so she would know what was happening in my personal pod of people.

Previously, DD had explained to me that, contrary to Logan's advice, it's better to message people rather than place a phone call directly. "When you phone someone, it puts them on the spot. They have to decide whether to pick up, or let the call go to voicemail. A text message lets them respond when they are available." DD's advice is always solid.

I knew that Nina would know what the ventilator does for Lucy. When Logan told me about it, I just nodded my head and pretended I understood what was going on. I had some ideas, yet didn't really know, and certainly what I thought didn't matter to

Logan. He was clearly quite upset with these developments. No smiles today.

"It's stressful for sure," Logan sighed while he hugged me hard. "Shane, I'm so glad you are here for me to talk to. I don't know what I'd do without you."

Myself, I don't get stressed out the way Logan does. For one thing, I don't know how to do it. The virus lockdown and isolation doesn't bother me. I don't know enough about stress anyway. Probably recently coming out of the coma makes me this way. "Don't sweat the small stuff," my sister says. "And, believe me, most stuff is small!"

Lucy died. *Five* days after they put her on a ventilator, she died. Her heart stopped beating. Nina says that the ventilator only helps the lungs but doesn't do anything for the heart. And in the end, it was heart failure that caused Lucy's death. "She died alone, no family, nothing. *Lucy died alone.*"

I was baffled about it all. Lucy was the first person I knew personally to die from the COVID-19 virus. The television and YouTube shows thousands of people dying, but Lucy's death was a direct hit to our group. "It's not abstract anymore."

Logan said there wouldn't be a public funeral or anything because of the government health officer's orders. She says there will not be any large, medium, or even small gatherings for fear of spreading the virus. "Maybe we will do some kind of ceremony or memorial down line."

Lucy was cremated. Her ashes are being held in storage in an urn at the crematorium for the time being. In the spring, or maybe summer, Logan says the family will hold an outdoor celebration of life, or something like that kind of rituals thing. Also, Logan says, of course, *we all have to go.*

Nina, on the other hand, who has the ultimate say over what concerns me, says she'll let me know whether I should go. "Timing is everything."

There has been some talk about lowering Lucy's urn into the ground over Zoom internet broadcast. "Lots of people are doing Zoom burials these days," according to the funeral folks. Logan said some family members were open to the idea. Wendy wasn't.

Nina says, "We had a nice ceremony of life when our parents died in the Kelowna car crash."

"I don't remember," I said shrugging my shoulders, and feeling bad about it.

Nina reached out, tenderly touched my shoulders, "Don't worry about it. We've got other stuff to be concerned about."

"Okay." I raised eyebrows with a smile. No argument from me, but I couldn't help but wonder what the other stuff was that we were concerned about. Guess it develops as we roll along. Maybe I'll figure it out. Maybe someone will tell me. Whatever.

DD often says, "Just let sleeping dogs alone."

And she explained that concept's content in a way I understood.

Glad I'm in DD's bubble.

"Don't poke the bear."

"Play with the bull, you'll get the horn."

Today is Blursday

"Things work well when we all do our part."
~Dr. Anneliese Robbens (1938 – 2017)

Today is Blursday.

Nowadays all the days blend together. I can't for certain tell one day from another, unless I check a secondary source. "It's the *new normal.*" So they all say. No worries, however, Randal gave me all the required answers should they make me take a mental status exam. I'm not completely crazy.

"You must know your name, age, day of the week, and where you are? Don't worry if you don't get them all correct. Fake it 'till you make it."

Lockdown life in relative isolation is what we've been doing for a while now. I never went to movie theatres anyway. Restaurants, well, it's takeout time these days. No one dines indoors anymore. It's too risky. People are dying.

So, you know, we've been back from India for a few months, but sometimes when I'm sleeping it still seems like we are going to wake up somewhere in India. It still feels like it was yesterday we were roaming around the Taj Mahal, Golden Temple, and the Agra Fort. I miss the food, smells, and cacophony of it all. All those people, I miss them. Randal never did get over the street noise.

For days and daze, I sat beside Randal Reilly on airplanes, cars, and he liked taking buses. We talked about everything. Dream interpretations, consciousness and the unconscious mind matters were favourite discussions. I can hold my own. I can debate. Traveling with him turned out to be a lot more fun than I would have ever thought. At first, I didn't want to travel with him, but when my brother *paid* me big bucks to be his guide I succumbed to cash.

These days due to COVID-19, I don't see Randal every day anymore, although I do talk, email or video him practically every day, sometimes twice a day. He's the same. This shelter stay at home quarantine stuff doesn't seem to faze him. Randal's quite malleable.

My brother Raj *insists* on calling him Uncle R and will likely continue to do so forever.

"He's not *your* uncle, Raj!" I've told him a trillion times.

"He is to me, and that's all that matters," Raj replies!

Randal and I bonded. We became good friends while traveling through India. Even so, our trip ended abruptly when COVID-19 started spreading across the planet. We were deep in the Punjab when the virus first stated spreading like wildfire.

We all had to return to Canada quickly. Even though my brother, Raj, and Amelia hold more than an adequate supply of liquid cash, and cryptocurrency, India was not where we wanted to be with an approaching pandemic. "It's a small fragile planet." Raj explained to me with some anxiety.

Flights out of India were all getting cancelled. Amelia and Mr. Meyers got us all out on one of his private airplanes. Because we were travelling on a private plane, we didn't have to go through the regular airport crowds, customs and border guard hassles at either end. We were lucky. Some acquaintances we knew were still stuck in New Delhi for a while longer. "We can't save everyone," my brother would say, "only direct family members and *close* friends are our immediate responsibility." Raj's boundaries get rigid. "The government will help those guys get home."

Amelia had us all divided into travel pods. It worked. We all got back home without too much difficulty. Randal and I said goodbye at the airport. His wife took him home.

I'm back living with my parents. Raj, Amelia, and baby David moved in with Amelia's mother, Annette. She has a big house and enjoys looking after David. Raj can work anywhere with an internet connection.

Prior to leaving India I had heard some raised voices coming out of Raj and Amelia's bedroom. Raj *seldom*, if ever, raises his voice. However, Amelia informed him that she had decided to return to the hospital where she was an intern. Amelia was determined to do frontline medical work. That was, of course, in addition to her research lab work, and motherly duties.

I think Amelia is amazing.

Caitlyn and Autocorrect (Carol Wilson) broke up. Caitlyn is back living with her parents, too. We've reconnected. It's good

Kelsey and her friend from Puerto Rico, Sojo, also got back to Vantown on one of Mr. Meyers's airplanes. Sojo was supposed to go back to Calgary, but she's sticking around for a while.

The university has shut down all classes. The place became a ghost town. Everything is done online with virtual learning. It sucks severely! I miss going to classes with my friends. I didn't start drinking coffee until university. Between classes we would slurp some java at our favourite hangout called 'The Barn Café.' It was once a spot for agriculture students—not anymore.

Raj keeps saying the pandemic will end when enough people have been vaccinated. Herd immunity is the goal.

Amelia says she is not so sure about the efficacy of the vaccination promises but prefers to wear an optimistic hat.

Me, I have no idea about anything other than I miss my friends, restaurants, drinks, parties, dating, traveling, regular life and having fun.

Having said that, however, millions and millions of people have died from the virus. That is the saddest part of the whole thing. Death.

Raj says my main job these days is to keep our parents safe and alive, "Parm, keep them close. Don't let them die from coronavirus."

"What," I chortled, "since when did you feel these parental concerns?"

He just laughed, "Heh, what can I say, they're our parents, foibles and all."

"Have you made peace with Pops?"

"No, we'll always be how we are. I have learned how to deal with it."

"Ya, guess that's for the best."

"You two are more alike than you realize."

"No, in the end it doesn't matter. The family tree will bend, but we haven't broken.'

"Yet."

"No, not yet."

Part Seven

POST COMATOSE

"They who dream by day are cognizant
of many things which escape those who
only dream by night."
~Edgar Allen Poe (1809 – 1849)

Out of the Picture

"Mother nature won't be predicable, so no use us trying."
~Marian Martin (1927 – 2012)

Understanding the passage of time still is perplexing for me.

Seems like yesterday when I was in the hospital there were always lots and lots of doctors, nurses, and special people popping into my room to ask questions and check on how I was doing. Charts, machines and tests all the time.

Then Logan and his father decided it was better for me to be out of the hospital and move into their coach house. Doctors then made 'house calls.' They came to *our* place. Some came by bicycle, some came by car, and some even took the bus. Now it's all run through the Zoom computer screen. Logan made me a phony tropical ocean background. Everyone on the call is in a checkerboard setup box.

I've learned to play checkers with Logan's daughter. It's good. Sometimes she cheats. Logan taught her the game. Banny taught me. We use her modified evolving rules.

~

So, all the experts say I have entered into a *post comatose* condition these days. My sister is a *player,* according to Logan. She says labels are ancillary to prognosis. "A differential diagnosis doesn't necessarily need to be debilitating. Problem solving is our goal."

Okay, fine with me. I didn't even know I had problems. Really, truth is I'm just living day-to-day. And I guess it's okay. Doesn't matter anyway. I don't know any different.

My sister, Logan, and all the guys have contributed to assembling a large photo library that has been loaded on to all my electronic devices. Now I've got lots of pics. If I click on the thumbnail, it goes full screen, the date and where the pic was taken appears on the top of the screen. Logan says we will annotate titles and captions later. Theoretically, the plan is these pics will help jog my memories and cognitive processing capacity.

There are some sweet baby pics of Nina, me, and our parents. Some family adventures. Not everyone is smiling all the time. I got pics of the guys and me riding bikes, camping and swimming. Nothing but smiles in those pics.

"You know, Shane," Logan started his instructional speech drone delivery, "you were in a coma for thirteen months. Before that you were in a couple different prisons. Before that you were behaving a bit like a wild and crazy guy. So, you know, there are some time gaps. You missed out on some things. Life rolled on, things happened, birthdays, events *where you are not in the picture."*

"Okay," seemed the right thing to reply, but suddenly Logan bursts into tears. He started crying quite loudly. The shaking convulsive kind of crying.

"When you were in the hospital, I thought you were a goner. They kept saying you might not come *out* of the coma. Before that they said you might have to go to jail for a while. You *killed* two guys. And before that you and I were not getting along as good as we should have. You were difficult to talk to back then."

"Sorry about that," I thought that was a good thing to say to Logan.

"No, no, I'm sorry I didn't take better care of you when you needed it. I should've been a better friend. I should've been there when you needed me."

Nina said the same thing, more or less, but she didn't shed tears over the gap in time, or the gap's cause. Nina is even kneeled. She's not as high strung as Logan. Nina says, "Etiology is overrated. More important is what you do about it."

Sure, she should know, she's a licensed expert. And that's as cool as it can get as far as I can figure. Nina knows things. I'm so happy she's in my corner. Compared to Nina, I'm a mental midget. Of course, Logan says we don't talk about midgets anymore because it is now quite politically incorrect. So, it's good I'm not saying stuff out loud but only in my brain. Nurse DD calls that verbal mediation, and that's a good thing. "Practice thinking about thinking, okay."

Yes, good idea, I started spending time thinking about thinking, rather than impulsively plunging forward. Look before you leap sort of thing. I'm with that plan for sure.

~

Guy Charles Clark (1942 – 2016) wrote a song saying, "My favourite picture of you is the one where you're staring straight into the lens. It's just a Polaroid shot, someone took on the spot, no beginning no end."

~

I appear in lots of pictures nowadays. I started sending selfies to folks. Nina says, "Send more."

Remorse – Slice or Shank

Grant Woods (1952 – 1969) said,
"Stay away from people with hair-triggered tempers."

I got a letter from Trevor Chapman.

Nina delivered it. "You received a letter from Trevor Chapman."

"Okay."

Nina handed me a battered envelope. "I read it already. It's okay."

"Thanks, that's good, I guess."

The letter was addressed to me in care of my lawyer's office.

First off, I searched my memory bank, but the name Trevor Chapman meant *nothing* to me. Turns out Trevor was one of the prison guards that smashed my head into the concrete floor in the Saskatchewan prison. Something I did made him angry.

Currently, Trevor is actively participating in a twelve-step counselling program. Trevor is in a rehab recovery program. He has issues with anger management, alcohol, domestic violence, and bad behaviour. He got fired from his prison guard job for smashing my head into the concrete floor. Trevor's lawyer from the guard's union got acquitted of the assault. He didn't have to go to jail or anything. Trevor got some sort of Saskatchewan probation with counselling conditions.

Trevor's counsellor contacted my lawyers to explain that as part of his twelve-step therapy program stuff he had to write a remorse letter to me. Making amends was important for Trevor's personal growth.

That's the deal with Trevor writing a letter. In turn, my lawyer gave the letter to Nina, and she brought it to me. I don't get much paper mail, mostly email. Snail mail has the physical component that is missing from email, according to Logan's father.

This was a long letter. Trevor's handwriting was almost like what Nina calls calligraphy. I read the letter. My reading skills are adequate, but nothing like Nina's skills. She can read between the lines. I'm not so good at that. Everything's literal for me.

Trevor said he was sorry for putting me in a coma. He asked for my forgiveness.

I believed him. His letter seemed sincere. I showed the letter to Logan. Ordinarily, Logan is less than forgiving, yet this time he said. "Well, it's not as though we have *never* fucked up, eh?"

"People in glass houses shouldn't throw stones."

"Yeah, and they should get dressed in the basement, too."

Logan just shrugged. I didn't get it but didn't let on so. A lot of humour is deeper than I can dive, especially with Logan. He's the funniest guy he knows.

Because of COVID restrictions, Trevor could not meet with me in person like his counsellor thought important. Logan said, "No problem, just like everything else these days, I will make arrangements, so we'll do it over the computer Zoom call."

Next, Logan did a detailed job explaining how remorse works. I never knew the difference between real remorse and phony boloney remorse. Logan knows the difference.

He pointed his finger at me, "Remember when we were in the fifth grade at Dunbar Beach Middle School?"

"No, sorry Logan," I re-explained, "my memory is episodic without sequential anchors."

"Right, ya, I knew that. No problem." He flashed his famous ear-to-ear smile. "Phony boloney remorse worked like this: we got caught climbing up onto the roof of the school's annex. We were trying to get the ball that Ned had kicked up there."

"Why did Ned do that?"

"It was an accident, the ball got away on him. He shanked it and kicked too hard. Any of us could have done the same thing. There by the grace of Zeus go I." Logan bowed his head and rolled his eyes.

"So, there we were, up on the roof, admiring the panoramic view, looking out at Kitsilano Beach, when all of a sudden, the skylight door pops open to the roof, and the Vice Principal, Mrs. Pritchard, emerges. We could see she was in a *mood.*"

"What kinda mood could we see?" I had to ask.

Logan laughed, "A less than pleased mood."

He went on to explain how the *faux remorse principle* worked. Logan knew Mrs. Pritchard's husband was a well-known Eagle Scout. Additionally, Logan knew Mrs. Pritchard was an *avid* golfer. "Those two key concepts got us out of the predicament."

"What was our predicament, again?"

"We were in trouble. Not big trouble or anything, just middle school hijinks trouble."

Logan explained how he told Mrs. Pritchard, "*Scout's honour,* we are so sincerely sorry about climbing up onto the roof. We will *never, ever* do anything dangerous again."

Mrs. Pritchard scowled, shook her head, but I continued, "It's just like golfing with my father. I get all stressed out and either slice the shot or shank it. It's so frustrating. My father's disappointment doesn't help either because I slow his game down."

Logan smiled, then I made my voice quiver, "Oh boy, oh boy, I sure hope we are not in trouble, Mrs. Pritchard. My father will be awfully angry. For sure he will ground me and make me miss the tournament this weekend."

"What happened?" I asked.

"Well, even though Mrs. Pritchard knew it was phony baloney remorse, she let us off the hook. Everyone knows phony remorse is better than no remorse."

"Do you still play golf?" I asked.

"No, of course not. I never played golf. Previously, when we were in Mrs. Pritchard's office for something or other, I noticed all her golf chotskies. In my mind I filed that knowledge knowing it may be useful someday. It was."

"It was?"

"Yes, it was," he chuckled, "got us out of the ball on the roof dilemma."

Out of courtesy, Logan asked Nina if she wanted to be with us and attend the virtual meeting with Trevor Chapman over the computer Zoom thing. Nina said she was certain we'd be fine on our own as a duet.

"Nina is busier than we will ever be," Logan explained.

"Ya, she's a hard worker, for sure. She has projects."

"Projects!"

Logan is computer proficient. He pushed some buttons, muttered stuff, and then proclaimed, "Alright, we're connected. Audio and video set, unmuted, here we go. Hello Trevor, I'm Logan, and here's Shane."

I raised my hand, waved hello, and wobbled my head, we're ready to talk. "Hi, I'm Shane."

Really, I didn't know what to expect when we met with Trevor. For one thing, I didn't expect he'd do so much crying. Previously, I thought Trevor was supposed to be a tough guy, macho man. Without a doubt, he was clearly sorry for putting me in a coma. I got that part.

Trevor had some other people from his counselling group sitting with him in the room's background. I understood they were there for therapeutic moral support. Later Logan said they were there to make sure Trevor followed through with what he was supposed to do. Logan says he's susceptible to peer pressure, too.

We spoke with Trevor for close to an hour. It was okay. Don't know if all this was for him or me, but it didn't matter. Logan poked me a couple times when he thought I was supposed to say something. I didn't know what to say other than, "I'm getting better, Trevor. I got lots of help. You take care, see you sometime down line."

We all waved goodbye, and that was that.

"Justice is a relative thing to think about, eh?" Logan looked up at the ceiling and whistled softly.

"How so?" I asked.

"Well, dunno, because there's the idea of criminal justice, yet our buddy, Raj, says karmic justice supersedes politics and religion."

"What level was our meeting with Trevor?"

Logan scrunched his forehead, shrugged, and said, "Dunno exactly, but without a doubt, you know Trevor wishes he could re-play the incident with you and *not* do that again."

"Ya, me too."

"What would you do different with Trevor?"

"No, not Trevor!" I explained, "Trent, wish I hadn't killed Declan Downes and Trent McKinney. Wish *that* could be a do-over. Nina tells me to let it go and move on to other endeavours. Don't stumble over something in your past."

Logan made a mutter noise that I couldn't decode. "Do you remember Harpreet Dhaliwal?" Logan asked.

"No, not really." I explained, "I've seen lots of photos of he and me, yet I don't know what the deal was with us. Nina says Harpreet was my friend. He had a brain injury but died young from *natural causes.*"

Looked like Logan was going to get weepy again. He gets glassy eyes.

Logan sniffled, wiped his eyes, "Harpreet insisted you were his best friend *ever.* Harpreet always said, Shane's the absolute nicest person he's *ever* known."

"That's nice."

"Harpreet wished he and Banerjee Malik had never tried the suicide pact project. He wished that could've been a do-over. It was an impulsive mistake. You saved his life, but Banny was already dead when we got there."

"Nina told me the story a few times, but she says I should not be so susceptible to *planted* memory stuff."

"Well, whatever, Nina knows best."

"Logan, can you arrange for me to talk to Trent and Declan's families, like we did today with Trevor?"

"What," he scrunched his face. "Why do you want to talk to those people? It's over and done."

"Wanna say I'm sorry for killing Trent and Declan."

"You *already* did that in court before sentencing."

"I did," shaking my head, "I don't remember."

"Yes, you did."

"We'll, I'd like to talk to them again then. Can you set it up?"

"I'll have to ask my dad, Nina, and their lawyers. You might have some legal exposure doing something like that. I'll get started, but I'm going to need their help and permission."

"Legal exposure?"

"Yes, I don't want them to civil court sue you because of legal exposure, wrongful death or something."

"That's okay," I assured him. "Nina says I got lots of money because of inheritance, and Ned's mother settled our lawsuit with the Saskatchewan and federal governments for my injuries, pain and suffering stuff."

"Whatever," he raised his palms, "I'll get on it, and get back to you straight away. It can't be too difficult to finagle."

"Thanks."

Legal Exposure

"Yes, I guess swearing at the school's principal was not a good thing to do, but you know she started it."
~Gene Blue Lonechild (1983 – 2011)

On my private number cell phone, the little corner icon indicated —voicemail. Not many people have this number.

I pushed the speaker button:

"Hello, this is Gerry Meyers calling for Annette Reilly. Briefly, my son Logan, and Shane Bighill want to set up a virtual meeting with the families of Trent McKinney and Declan Downes. Shane wishes to express further remorse for his behaviour some years ago. They got this idea recently after a therapy session with one of Shane's previous prison guards. I said I'd seek your legal opinion on this matter before they could proceed to the next level. What legal exposure are we looking at with Shane's intentions? Please call me back at your convenience. Thanks."

I listened to Gerry's message, twice. Then I printed a pdf of the message to send to Amelia.

Although my tech savvy falls short of my children, I'm semi-competent for some of these things. Amelia and I had a large *falling out* over Shane's negotiated plea arrangement a few years ago. I feel like we have recovered to an acceptable level, yet I'm not pushing the envelope. Besides, Amelia and Gerry Meyers are friends. They worked together to get all our people out of India before the pandemic descended all over the planet and the lockdown began.

Below the pdf post I asked, "Amelia, I know you are busy, but could you deal with this? I don't know what tell them. What do you think?"

Less than two minutes passed when Amelia replied with a text saying: "Yes, mother, I've got this. I will call Gerry. If there's any legal exposure, we don't care. Shane can do whatever he wants. He's got all the support we can offer. Gerry is by nature, legally, a cautious guy, but he's cool. We are good here. Thanks. See You Later."

Whew, this reply alleviated any anxiety I had about everything. Currently, Amelia and I are close to copacetic, and that makes me feel happy. So, I thought I'd reply back. I know she does not like lengthy texts, so I simply said, "Thanks."

Her immediate response, "No problem."

I thought, terrific, this is not a problem for Amelia which is good, for me. I can use her problem-solving assistance. There's enough going on these days in my orbit without adding *more* problems. Besides, I'm tired. Exhaustingly tired.

There's a lot of this and that going on these days.

I'm awfully tired.

Chaucer and Patience

"Always drink upstream from the herd."
~Will Rogers (1879 – 1935)

I clearly remember back when I was in the hospital, Nurse DD would sit bedside, and read to me. I understood some stories, and not others. Poems were nice. The cadence of her voice seemed soothing. DD knew what the deal was in the hospital. Everyone else speculated.

DD used to read Geoffrey Chaucer's *The Canterbury Tales.* She was good with voices. "Cato needed to learn that patience is a virtue."

Nina says, historically, Logan is an impulsive, impatient person. Trying to explain why we need patience to him wasn't worthwhile. Logan's auditory hearing is adequate, but listening is another thing altogether.

Nina says, "Logan's a *ready, fire, aim,* kinda a guy." Personality and individual differences are important Nina explained. "Shane, you have to understand, Logan is Logan." She made a snorting noise, "He is, however, one of the best friends you could *ever* have. He's got your back."

Took a few days for Logan to start getting procedural directions and responses for our request to virtually meet with the families. "First, we've got to write letters to Trent and Declan's parents.

Sort of ice breaking like the way Trevor did when he set the virtual meeting up with you." Logan continued, "I've got their surface mail addresses. Unlike Trevor, we don't have to go through shrinks or lawyers. Dad says his lawyers are available and we could use them if we want. All we must do is just call. But we don't have to make the first volley a big deal. Just tell them what you want. We can't necessarily just expect a Zoom meeting is going to happen. Not everyone likes the Zoom thing."

"Alright," I gave him the thumbs up signal, "thanks Logan."

He set out some pens, notepad, and papers on the kitchen table, "You start writing what you are thinking. I'll come back later when you have finished, we will edit together. Take your time, there's no rush."

I smiled, thinking to myself, Logan seems patient enough now that the ball has started rolling. Next, we will see how he reacts if the ball doesn't roll as fast as he would wish. I gave him the thumbs up signal, and said, "I will type something out first before I put pen to paper."

"Sure, whatever, old school or dictates are good at this point. And you've talked to Nina about this, right?"

I shrugged, "Yes, she's supportive, but doesn't want a high-level intensity involvement because of her lab work schedule. She says to call her if we need her."

"Good, that's good. I know the time when you and Harpreet went to meet with Banny's family so he could say he was sorry about her dying, Nina got quite upset."

"Why was she upset?"

"Because you guys were trespassing, and the police were called, and everything went badly. We watched on television. Nina never liked it when you got in trouble with the cops."

"Why?"

"Because it meant she would have to bail you out of whatever predicament you put yourself in. She's your twin sister. It's always been her job to look out for you."

A few days passed, we had some back-and-forth letter writing. In my opening *icebreaking* letter, I explained that I was sincerely sorry for my behaviour and wished I had not taken the lives of Trent and Declan. I asked if they were interested in meeting with me, virtually, to talk.

Trent's family said no thanks and asked me to leave them alone.

Declan's mother and sister said they would meet with me virtually.

Declan's dad said no way was he interested in having anything to do with me—*ever.*

Eventually we settled on a date and convenient time to virtually meet with Delores and Sandra. Logan set the equipment up, got us connected, and sat beside me while we talked. He prepped me earlier making it clear that I was supposed to do the talking and he was there for *moral support* (whatever that meant).

I opened the session with some apologies. Delores and Sandra were, generally, forgiving with sympathetic understanding of my sincerity. They said they remembered me from all the various court appearances a few years ago. It was a long-drawn-out legal affair.

Again, I apologized and explained that there are large gaps in my long-term memory due to an incident while I was in the Saskatchewan prison. Consequently, "I unfortunately do not remember the court proceedings."

They said, yes, they knew about my situation from various media reports. "You have a very good lawyer," Sandra mentioned, nodding her head.

"Thanks," I didn't really know what to say, "Both Amelia and her mother are very committed to helping me. They have known me all my life."

"Well, we are happy to see you are recovering," Sandra continued to do most of the talking.

We did some more small talk, ending the first session with an agreement to do another one soon. We all waved goodbye.

The next time we met it was just Sandra and me. Logan was busy. Mrs. Downes was doing something. So, Sandra and I had a virtual meeting, just the two of us. It was good. We connected.

Sandy and I did some back-and-forth emails, texts, and stuff, then we decided we might as well get together *in person* for lunch.

We've both been vaccinated, twice.

Next week, either Tuesday or Friday, we're meeting at Tanaka's Sushi Shoppe on Main Street.

I called Nina and asked if she wanted to come along, but she said she's busy. We invited Sandy's mother. She's not sure about her schedule. Maybe she'll join us. Either way we're cool.

I love sushi.

Epilogue

"Shane's got a girlfriend."

"Really, who is she?"

"Sandy Downes, she's Declan's sister."

"Who is Declan?"

"He is one of the guys that Shane killed and got sent to prison."

"It's a weird world."

"Yeah, and COVID-19 is still raging!"

"Shane is vaccinated, right?

"Yes,"

"Well, we wish him well."

"We do indeed."

The End

Acknowledgements

"It is not easy bringing a book into this world."
~Richard Wagamese (1955 – 2017)

In 1967 John Lennon and Paul McCartney wrote it, Ringo sang it:

"With a Little Help from My Friends." Joe Cocker turned the song into an anthem at Woodstock.

A number of friends and family helped me put this book together. This is the place where I say thanks and acknowledge their help.

Some of this book, and good ideas generated, were written while we were staying uncle's ancestral home in Mehraj. Although I always think about travelling lighter, I never seem to do so. I showed up in the Punjab with lots of luggage, a Cowichian ukulele, laptop, tablet, and iPhone. I needed a new SIM card to serve as a 'hotspot' to power all the equipment while we travelled. Uncle Mohinder is a lawyer. He knew how to fill out the SIM card forms correctly. In India some government regulations and forms are complicated. Uncle Mohinder drove me all over his part of the Punjab to get the job done. This book owes uncle and cousin Ruby an enormous amount of gratitude for their hospitality, tolerance, and stories.

Previously, last time, when we stayed at Mehraj, Auntie Harjinder kept serving me endless roti, paratha, naan, saag, dhal and chai. I always said "thank you" profusely. Because I've been a marathon runner for the past thirty-five years, I'm a competent carbo loader. I could eat a lot of auntie's cooking.

Cousin Ruby confronted me saying, "John, my mother says I am to tell you *stop* saying shukria, dhannvaad, thanks, and whatever else it is you are saying. She enjoys serving you. It's her duty because you are a *family* guest."

In my defence, I explained, "Indeed, that may be so but please tell auntie that my mother sits on my shoulder like a little homunculus constantly reminding me about *good manners.* So, it's more about me than auntie. My mother worked hard teaching manners."

Auntie nodded her head with agreement, "You are known by your manners, not your name."

In this book there is a chapter about horses. My grandfather, Martin, taught me how to ride a horse (extensive eight minutes of instruction for an eight-year-old), conquer my fear of rooster attacks, and how to shoot a rifle at a chicken-eating coyote (my mother forbade farmlife firearms—gramps didn't care). He also taught me about coca cola. We would buy little bottles to guzzle in downtown Drumheller. Summer, those were the days.

Cody got a driver's license—a category L, Z, N or X. I don't know how the system works anymore. I told Cody about the day I turned sixteen. Of course, it snowed that day, but we jumped into my mum's 1962 baby blue T-bird and drove to the DMV. All the while she kept reminding: "Nobody passes the driver's test on their first try. Some people (no names mentioned) take three tries."

No problem, I was pronoid (opposite of paranoid), undeterred, and confident. I had been practicing all summer. Seriously, I could parallel park the Thunderbird with my eyes closed. Parallel parking was the Achilles part of the driving test. I knew that but was more than ready. All summer I had practiced parking by putting four buckets of dirt with poles inside. Two pails were curbside and two on the street. The T-bird approached the parking spot, I aligned the poles, and parked. Nothing to it I could do it—with my eyes closed.

I passed the test, first try. We celebrated with takeout chow mein, chicken fried rice, sweet and sour ribs. I've been driving every day since.

In this story I write about traffic in India. I could *never* drive in India. Cousin Neetu can drive. He's a pro! Neetu took time off work to drive us everywhere. We went to the Golden Temple, Pakistan border guard changing ceremonies, restaurants, relative's homes and all over the Punjab. The traffic freaked me out because I sat in the front passenger's seat. Neetu is a scientist and a very good driver. India has traffic. I can't drive in India.

I didn't have too much trouble driving in *rural* France.

Pulitzer Prize winner Carol Shields bought a four-hundred-year-old house in rural France. Her daughter, Anne Giardini, OC, OBC, QC, is such a good friend. Anne took the bus downtown to drop off the keys at the courthouse so we could stay at her home in France.

I sat at Carol's desk, wrote some pages, and drank French wine. It was a good time. Anne had explained the Carol Shields method of writing was to write something everyday. Some days are more productive than others. Just do what you can, don't worry about it.

2016, Anne and Nicholas Giardini wrote, *Startle and Illuminate.* I went to a reading at their house (Anne always has fabulous food). Anne and Nicholas did some readings. Anne talked about how her mother said it was important to do good work. More importantly, however, Carol says *do good.* Be a good person, do good things. That's Anne—she is one of the most generous people you could ever know. Anne does good work. Friends.

I didn't like working in the asbestos mine. That was a bad job.

A good job was when I worked with Dr. Gordon Hirabayashi. I was his teaching assistant. Unlike the mine, these working conditions were safe, pay scale was good, and I started drinking coffee at our staff meetings. Inarguably a very good job.

Gordon and I worked together on a social psychology course as well as one on race and ethnicity. Gordon was right-handed but could do a good left-handed layup on our basketball team. However, basketball notwithstanding, Gordon was skeptical about a master's thesis on left-handedness, middle children, and social psychology. So, he suggested his colleague, Andy Harrell, "Andy likes that type of research."

Indeed, Andy does favour innovations. Social psychology or legal research, Andy is an Ace.

If you should find yourself in Los Angeles needing a good lawyer. I can certainly recommend Dr. W. Andrew Harrell. He is left-handed (we never used the French term gauche, or old English cack-handedness).

In 1978, Andy got a new fancy *electric* typewriter. He handed down his *manual* Smith Corona and a box of ribbons. I wrote a thesis on that typewriter, and a novel called: *The Geriatric Joint.*

Andy was my thesis supervisor, and a power forward on our basketball team.

University of California, distinguished professor, Dr. H. Lee Swanson supervised my doctoral dissertation. Lee and I met every Thursday morning at 7:00. Lee taught me how to do signal detection analyses, time series covariance analyses, and *patience.*

When we (mostly Lee) thought a draught copy was adequate to circulate to the committee members, *hard* copies were printed and distributed. "Just be patient, they will give us their feedback in *due course.* You should always have another project to work on while we wait." Lee suggested. He always had a half dozen projects cooking. In addition to being a marvelous man, Lee is the most productive scholar I have ever known!

While we were waiting for dissertation committee feedback, I started writing some stories about accountants that ended up as a novel called *Crazy Cousins.*

1981, I was a schoolteacher in Cumberland, a small village on Vancouver Island. That was a good job.

In my novel *Cape Lazo,* there's a social studies teacher by the name of Mrs. Wagner. She's fictional, but in real life, Susan Wagner is the sweetest Australian I have ever known. Ever.

1991, when Sue Wagner was the BCASP (British Columbia Association of School Psychologists) President we worked together on a committee writing the first BCASP Code of Ethics. Well, Sue did most of the work. However, consistently generous, Sue credits the committee for the final product.

Susan Wagner was a proofreader for this book. Of course, any errors are mine. That said, Sue is a thorough and thoughtful reader. I can't thank her enough for all her help proofreading this book. Sue is such a good friend.

Special thanks to Vladimir Verano. This is the fifth novel Vlad has designed for me. Vlad is an artist. I appreciate his work tremendously.

John Dinning says, "Buy nice or buy twice."

Cody says, "Scientists are working hard these days."

Harbans say, "Just do what makes you happy.

About the Author

John Carter is a licensed psychologist, adj. prof. at UBC, a singer, and a slow paddler off the Mayne Island coast. *Shane's Coma* is his fifth novel.

CPSIA information can be obtained
at www.ICGtesting.com
Printed in the USA
LVHW011815170322
713551LV00006B/174